The

ESSENTIAL COLLECTION

#1 New York Times Bestselling Author

DEBBIE MACOMBER

Laughter In the RAIN

HARLEQUIN®
ESSENTIAL DEBBIE MACOMBER COLLECTION

Recycling programs
for this product may
not exist in your area.

ISBN-13: 978-0-373-47290-1

LAUGHTER IN THE RAIN

For questions and comments about the quality of this book, please contact us at CustomerService@Harlequin.com.

Printed in U.S.A.

DEBBIE MACOMBER

is a number one *New York Times* and *USA TODAY* best-selling author. Her books include *1225 Christmas Tree Lane, 1105 Yakima Street, A Turn in the Road, Hannah's List* and *Debbie Macomber's Christmas Cookbook,* as well as *Twenty Wishes, Summer on Blossom Street* and *Call Me Mrs. Miracle.* She has become a leading voice in women's fiction worldwide and her work has appeared on every major bestseller list, including those of the *New York Times, USA TODAY, Publishers Weekly* and *Entertainment Weekly.* She is a multiple award winner, and won the 2005 Quill Award for Best Romance. There are more than one hundred million copies of her books in print. Two of her Harlequin MIRA Christmas titles have been made into Hallmark Channel Original Movies, and the Hallmark Channel has launched a series based on her bestselling Cedar Cove series. For more information on Debbie and her books, visit her website, www.debbiemacomber.com.

One

"I'm so late. I'm so late."

The words were like a chant in Abby Carpenter's mind with every frantic push of the bike pedals. She was late. A worried glance at her watch when she paused at the traffic light confirmed that Mai-Ling would already be in Diamond Lake Park, wondering where Abby was. Abby should have known better than to try on that lovely silk blouse, but she'd seen it in the store's display window and couldn't resist. Now she was paying for the impulse.

The light turned green and Abby pedaled furiously, rounding the corner to the park entrance at breakneck speed.

Panting, she stopped in front of the bike stand and secured her lock around a concrete post. Then she ran across the lush green lawn to the picnic tables, where she normally met Mai-Ling. Abby felt a rush of relief when she spotted her.

Mai-Ling had recently immigrated to Minneapolis from Hong Kong. As a volunteer for the World Literacy Movement, Abby was helping the young woman learn to read English. Mai-Ling caught sight of her and waved eagerly. Abby, who'd been meeting her every Saturday afternoon for the past two months, was impressed by her determination to master English.

"I'm sorry I'm late," Abby apologized breathlessly.

Mai-Ling shrugged one shoulder. "No problem," she said with a smile.

That expression demonstrated how

quickly her friend was adapting to the American way of speaking—and life.

Mai-Ling started to giggle.

"What's so funny?" Abby asked as she slid off her backpack and set it on the picnic table.

Mai-Ling pointed at Abby's legs.

Abby looked down and saw one red sock and one that was blue. "Oh, dear." She sighed disgustedly and sat on the bench. "I was in such a rush I didn't even notice." No wonder the salesclerk had given her a funny look. Khaki shorts, mismatched socks and a faded T-shirt from the University of Minnesota.

"I am laughing with you," Mai-Ling said in painstaking English.

Abby understood what she meant. Mai-Ling wanted to be sure Abby realized she wasn't laughing *at* her. "I know," she said as she zipped open the backpack and took out several workbooks.

Mai-Ling sat opposite Abby. "The man's here again," she murmured.

"Man?" Abby twisted around. "What man?"

Abby couldn't believe she'd been so unobservant. She felt a slight twinge of apprehension as she looked at the stranger. There was something vaguely familiar about him, and that bothered her. Then she remembered—he was the same man she'd seen yesterday afternoon at the grocery store. Had he been following her?

The man turned and leaned against a tree not more than twenty feet away, giving her a full view of his face. His tawny hair gleamed in the sunshine that filtered through the leaves of the huge elm. Beneath dark brows were deep-set brown eyes. Even from this distance Abby could see their intense expression. His rugged face seemed to be all angles and planes. He was attractive in an earthy way that would appeal to a lot of women and Abby was no exception.

"He was here last week," Mai-Ling said. "And the week before. He was watching you."

"Funny, I don't remember seeing him," she murmured, unable to disguise her discomfort.

"He is a nice man, I think. The animals like him. I am not worried about him."

"Then I won't worry, either," Abby said with a shrug as she handed Mai-Ling the first workbook.

In addition to being observant, Mai-Ling was a beautiful, sensitive and highly intelligent woman. Sometimes she became frustrated with her inability to communicate, but Abby was astonished at her rapid progress. Mai-Ling had mastered the English alphabet in only a few hours and was reading Level Two books.

A couple of times while Mai-Ling was

reading a story about a woman applying for her first job, Abby's attention drifted to the stranger. She watched in astonishment as he coaxed a squirrel down the trunk of the tree. He pulled what appeared to be a few peanuts from his pocket and within seconds the squirrel was eating out of his hand. As if aware of Abby's scrutiny, he stood up and sauntered lazily to the nearby lakeshore. The instant he appeared, the ducks squawked as though recognizing an old friend. The tall man took bread crumbs from a sack he carried and fed them. Lowering himself to a crouch, he threw back his head and laughed.

Abby found herself smiling. Mai-Ling was right; this man had a way with animals—and women, too, if her pounding heart was anything to judge by.

A few times Mai-Ling faltered over a word, and Abby paused to help her.

The hour sped by, and soon it was time for the young woman to meet her bus.

Abby walked Mai-Ling to the busy street and waited until she'd boarded, cheerfully waving to Abby from the back of the bus.

Pedaling her bicycle toward her apartment, Abby's thoughts again drifted to the tall, good-looking stranger. She had to admit she was enthralled. She wondered if he was attracted to her, too, since apparently he came to the park every week while she was there. But maybe she wasn't the one who attracted him; perhaps it was Mai-Ling. No, she decided. Mai-Ling had noticed the way the handsome stranger studied Abby. He was interested *in her.* Great, she mused contentedly; Logan Fletcher could do with some competition.

Abby pulled into the parking lot of her low-rise apartment building and climbed off her bike. Automatically she reached for her backpack, which she'd placed on the rack behind her, to get the apartment keys. Nothing. Surprised, Abby turned around to look for it. But it wasn't there. Obviously she'd left it at the park. Oh, no! She exhaled in frustration and turned, prepared to go and retrieve her pack.

"Looking for this?" A deep male voice startled Abby and her heart almost dropped to her knees. The bike slipped out from under her and she staggered a few steps before regaining her balance.

"Don't you know better than to sneak up on someone like that? I could have…" The words died on her lips as she whirled around to face the stranger. With her mouth hanging half open she stared into the deepest brown eyes she'd ever seen—the man from the park.

Her tongue-tied antics seemed to amuse him, but then it could have been her mismatched socks. "You forgot this." He handed her the backpack. Speechless, Abby took it and hugged it to her stomach. She felt grateful…and awkward.

She started to thank him when another thought came to mind.

"How'd…how'd you know where I live?" The words sounded slightly scratchy, and she cleared her throat.

He frowned. "I've frightened you, haven't I?"

"How'd you know?" She repeated the question less aggressively. He hadn't scared her. If anything, she felt a startling attraction to him, to the sheer force of his masculinity. Logan would be shocked. For that matter, so was she. But up close, this man was even more appealing than he'd been at a distance.

"I followed you," he said simply.

"Oh." A thousand confused emotions dashed through her mind. He was so good-looking that Abby couldn't manage another word.

"I didn't mean to scare you," he said, regret in his voice.

"You didn't," she hurried to assure him. "I have an overactive imagination."

Shaking his head, he thrust his hands into his pants pockets. "I'll leave before I do any more damage."

"Please don't apologize. I should be thanking you. There's a Coke machine around the corner. Would you like to—"

"I've done enough for one day." Abruptly he turned to go.

"At least tell me your name." Abby didn't know where the request came from; it tumbled from her lips before she'd even formed the thought.

"Tate." He tossed it over his shoulder as he stalked away.

"Bye, Tate," she called as he opened his car door. When he glanced her way, she lifted her hand. "And thanks."

A smile curved his mouth. "I like your socks," he returned.

Pointedly she looked down at the mismatched pair. "I'm starting a new trend," she said with a laugh.

Standing beside her bike, Abby waited until Tate had driven away.

* * *

Later that night, Logan picked her up and they had hamburgers, then went to a movie. Logan's obligatory good-night kiss was…pleasant. That was the only way Abby could describe it. She had the impression that Logan kissed her because he always kissed her goodnight. To her dismay, she had to admit that there'd never been any driving urgency behind his kisses. They'd been dating almost a year and the mysterious Tate was capable of stirring more emotion with a three-minute conversation than Logan had all evening. Abby wasn't even sure why they continued to date. He was an accountant whose office was in a building near hers. They had many of the same friends, and did plenty of things together, but their relationship was in a rut. The time had come to add a little spice to her life and Abby knew exactly where that spice would be coming from….

After Logan had left, Abby settled into the overstuffed chair that had once belonged to her grandfather, and picked up a new thriller she'd bought that week.

Dano, her silver-eyed cat, crawled into her lap as Abby opened the book. Absently she stroked the length of his spine. Her hand froze in midstroke as she discovered the hero's name: Logan. Slightly unnerved, she dropped the book and jumped up from her chair to look for the remote. Turning on the TV, she told herself she shouldn't feel guilty because she felt attracted to another man. The first thing she saw on the screen was a commercial for Logan Furniture's once-a-year sofa sale. Abby stared at the flashing name and hit the off button. This was crazy! Logan wouldn't care if she was interested in someone else. He might even be grateful. Their relationship was based on friendship and had progressed to romance, a romance that was more about routine than passion. If Abby was attracted to another man, Logan would be the first to step aside. He was like that—warm, unselfish, accommodating.

Her troubled thoughts on Saturday evening were only the beginning. Tate dominated every waking minute, which just went to prove how limited her social life really was. She liked Logan, but Abby longed for some excitement. He was so staid—yes, that was the word. *Staid.* Solid as a rock, and about as imaginative.

Logan came over to her apartment on Sunday afternoon, which was no surprise. He always came over on Sunday afternoons. They usually did something together, but never anything very exciting. More often than not Abby went over to his house and made dinner. Sometimes they watched a DVD. Or they played a game of backgammon, which he generally won. During the summer they'd ride their bikes, some of their most pleasant dates had been spent in

Diamond Lake Park. Logan would lie on the grass and rest his head in her lap while she read whatever thriller or mystery she was currently devouring.

They'd been seeing each other so often that the last time they had dinner at her parents', Abby's father had suggested it was time they thought about getting married. Abby had been mortified. Logan had laughed and changed the subject. Later, her mother had tactfully reminded Abby that he might not be the world's most exciting man, but he was her best prospect. However, Abby couldn't see any reason to rush into marriage. At twenty-six, she had plenty of time.

"I thought we'd bike around the park," Logan said.

The day was gloriously sunny and although Abby wished Logan had proposed something more inventive, the idea *was* appealing. She enjoyed the feel of the breeze in her hair and the sense of exhilaration that came with rapid movement.

"Hi!" Abby and Logan were greeted by Patty Martin just inside the park's boundaries. "How's it going?"

"Fine," Logan answered for them as they braked to a stop. "How about you?"

Patty had recently started to work in the same office building as Logan, which was how Abby had met her. Although Abby didn't know her well, she'd learned that Patty was living with her sister. They'd talked briefly at lunch one day, and Abby had invited her to join an office-league softball team she and Logan had played in last summer.

"I'm fine, too," Patty answered shyly and looked away.

In some ways she reminded Abby of Mai-Ling, who hadn't said more than a few words to her the first couple of weeks they'd worked together. Only as they came to know each other did Mai-Ling blossom. Abby herself had never been shy. The world was her friend, and she felt certain Patty would soon be comfortable with her, too.

"I can't talk now. I saw you and just wanted to say hello. Have fun, you two," Patty murmured and hurried away.

Confused, Abby watched her leave. The girl looked like a frightened mouse as she scurried across the grass. The description was more than apt. Patty's drab brown hair was pulled back from her face and styled unattractively. She didn't wear makeup and was so shy it was difficult to strike up a conversation.

After biking around the lake a couple of times, they stopped to get cold drinks. As they rested on a park bench, Logan slipped an affectionate arm around Abby's shoulders. "Have I told you that you look lovely today?"

The compliment astonished Abby; there were times she was convinced Logan didn't notice anything about her. "Thank you. I might add that you're looking very good yourself," she said with twinkling eyes, then added, "but I won't. No need for us both to get conceited."

Logan smiled absently as they walked their bikes out of the park. His expression was oddly distant; in some ways he hadn't been himself lately, but she couldn't put her finger on anything specific.

"Do you mind if we cut our afternoon short?" he asked unexpectedly.

He didn't offer an explanation, which surprised Abby. They'd spent most Sunday afternoons together for the past year. More surprising—or maybe not, considering her recent boredom with Logan— was the fact that Abby realized she didn't care. "No, that shouldn't be any problem. I've got a ton of laundry to do anyway."

Back at her apartment, Abby spent the rest of the afternoon doing her nails, feeling lazy and ignoring her laundry. She talked to her mother on the phone and promised to stop by sometime that week. Abby had been on her own ever since college. Her job as receptionist at an orthopedic clinic had developed with time and specialized training into a position as an X-ray technician. The advancement had included a healthy pay increase—enough to start saving for a place of her own. In the meanwhile, she relished her independence, enjoying her spacious ground-floor apartment, plus the satisfactions of her job and her volunteer work.

Several times over the next few days, Abby discovered herself thinking about Tate. Their encounter had been brief, but had left an impression on her. He was the most exciting thing that had happened to her in months.

"What's the matter with you?" Abby admonished herself. "A handsome man gives you a little attention and you don't know how to act."

Dano mewed loudly and weaved between her bare legs, his long tail tickling her calves. It was the middle of June and the hot summer weather had arrived.

"I wasn't talking to you." She leaned over to pet the cat. "And don't tell me you're hungry. I know better."

"Meow."

"You've already had your dinner."

"Meow. Meow."

"Don't you talk to me in that tone of voice. You hear?"

"Meow."

Abby tossed him the catnip mouse he loved to hurl in the air and chase madly after. Logan had gotten it for Dano. With his nose in the air, the cat ignored his toy and sauntered into Abby's room, jumping up to sit on the windowsill, his back to her. He ignored Abby, obviously pining after whatever he could see outside. In some obscure way, Abby felt that she was doing the same thing to Logan and experienced a pang of guilt.

Since it was an older building, the

apartments didn't have air-conditioning, so Abby turned on her large fan. Then, settling in the large overstuffed chair, she draped one leg over the arm and munched on an apple as she read. She was so engrossed in her thriller that when she glanced at her watch, she gasped in surprise. Her Tuesday evening painting class was in half an hour and Logan would arrive in less than fifteen minutes. He was always punctual, and although he seldom said anything, she could tell by the set of his mouth that he disliked it when she was behind schedule.

The "I'm late, I'm late" theme ran through her mind as she vaulted out of the chair, changed pants and rammed her right foot into her tennis shoe without untying the lace. Whipping a brush through her long brown hair, she searched frantically for the other shoe.

"It's got to be here," she told the empty room frantically. "Dano," she cried out in frustration. "Did you take my shoe?"

She heard a faint indignant "meow" from the bedroom.

On her knees she crawled across the carpet, desperately tossing aside anything in her path—a week-old newspaper, a scarf, a CD case, the mismatched pair of socks she'd worn last Saturday and a variety of other unimportant things.

She bolted to her feet when her apartment buzzer went off. Logan must be early.

She automatically let him into the building, threw open her door—and saw *Tate* standing in the hallway.

Abby felt the hot color seep up from her neck. He *would* come now, when she wasn't prepared and looking her worst.

He approached her apartment. "Hello," he said, staring down at her one bare foot. "Missing something?"

"Hello again." Her voice sounded unnaturally high. She bit her lip and tried to smile. "My shoe's gone."

"Walked away, did it?"

"You might say that. It was here a few minutes ago. I was reading and..." She dropped to her knees and lifted the skirting around the chair. There, in all its glory, was the shoe.

"Find it?" He was still in the doorway.

"Yes." She sat on the edge of the cushion and jerked her foot into the shoe.

"It might help if you untied the laces," he said, watching her with those marvelous eyes.

"I know, but I'm in a hurry." With her heel crushing the back of the shoe, Abby hobbled over to the door. "Come on in." She closed it behind him. "I'm—"

"Abby."

"Yes. How did you know?"

"I heard your friend say it at the park. And when I got to the lobby, I asked one of your neighbors." He frowned. "You should identify your guests before you let them in, you know."

"I know. I will. But I—was expecting someone else and…" Her words drifted off.

Smiling, he offered her his hand. "Tate Harding," he said.

A tingling sensation slipped up her arm at his touch.

Tate's hand was callused and rough from work. She successfully restrained her desire to turn it over and examine the palm. His handsome face was tanned from exposure to the elements. Tate was handsome, compellingly so.

"It looks as if I came at an inconvenient time."

"Oh, no," she hurried to assure him. She noticed that he'd released his grip, although she continued to hold her hand in midair. Self-consciously she lowered it to her side. "Sit down," she said, motioning toward her favorite chair. The hot color in her face threatened to suffocate her with its intensity.

Tate sat and lazily crossed his legs,

apparently unaware of the effect he had on her.

Abby was shocked by her own reaction. She'd dated a number of men. She was neither naive nor stupid. "Would you like something to drink?" she asked as she hastily retreated to the kitchen, not waiting for his answer. Pausing, she frantically prayed that for once, just once, Logan would be late. No sooner had the thought formed than she heard the apartment buzzer again. This time she listened to her speaker.

"Abby?"

Logan. Abby hesitated, but let him in.

Tate had stood and opened the door by the time she turned around. Logan had arrived. When he stepped inside, the two men eyed each other skeptically. A slight scowl drew Logan's brows together.

"Logan, this is Tate Harding. Tate, Logan Fletcher." Abby flushed uncomfortably and darted an apologetic look at them both.

"I thought we had a class tonight." Logan spoke somewhat defensively.

"This is my fault," Tate said, his gaze resting on Abby's face and for one heart-stopping moment on her softly parted lips. "I dropped by unexpectedly."

Logan's mouth thinned with displeasure and Abby pulled her eyes from Tate's. Logan had never been the jealous type, but then he'd never had reason or opportunity to reveal that side of his nature. Still, it surprised her. Abby hadn't considered this a serious relationship. It was more of a companionable one. Logan had understood and accepted that, or so she'd thought.

"I'll come back another time," Tate suggested. "You've obviously got plans with Logan."

"We're taking classes together," Abby rushed to explain. "I'm taking painting and Logan's studying chess. We drive there together, that's all."

Tate's smile was understanding. "I won't keep you, then."

"Nice to have met you," Logan stated, sounding as if he meant exactly the opposite.

Tate turned back and nodded. "Perhaps we'll meet again."

Logan nodded briskly. "Perhaps."

The minute Tate left Abby whirled around to face Logan. "That was so rude," she whispered fiercely. "For heaven's sake—you were acting like you owned me…like I was your property."

"Think about it, Abby," Logan said just as forcefully, also in a heated whisper. His dark eyes narrowed as he stalked to the other side of the room. "We've been dating exclusively for almost a year. I assumed that you would've developed some loyalty. I guess I was mistaken."

"Loyalty? Is that all our relationship means to you?" she demanded.

Logan didn't answer her. He walked

to the door and held it open, indicating that if she was coming she needed to do it now. Silently Abby followed him through the lobby and into the parking lot.

The entire way to the community center they sat without speaking. The hard set of Logan's mouth indicated the tight rein he had on his temper. Abby forced her expression to remain haughtily cold.

They parted in the hallway, Logan taking the first left while Abby continued down the hall. A couple of the women she'd become friends with greeted her, but Abby had difficulty responding. She took twice as long as normal setting up her supplies.

The class, which was on perspective, didn't go well, since Abby's attention kept returning to the scene with Logan and Tate. Logan was obviously jealous. He'd revealed more emotion in those few minutes with Tate than in the past twelve months. Logan tended to be serious and reserved, while she was more emotional and adventurous. They were simply mismatched. Like her socks—one red, one blue. Logan had become too comfortable in their relationship these last months, taking too much for granted. The time had come for a change, and after tonight he had to recognize that.

After class they usually met in the coffee shop beside the center. Logan was already in a booth when she arrived there.

Wordlessly, Abby slipped into the seat across from him. Folding her hands on the table, she pretended to study her nails, wondering if Logan was ever going to speak.

"Why are you so angry?" Abby finally asked. "I hardly know Tate. We only met a few days ago."

"How many times have you gone out with him?"

"None," Abby said righteously.

"But not because you turned him down." Logan shook his head grimly. "I saw the way you looked at him, Abby. It was all you could do to keep from drooling."

"That's not true," she denied vehemently—and realized he was probably right. She'd never been good at hiding her feelings. "I admit I find him attractive, but—"

"But what?" Logan taunted softly. "But you had this old boyfriend you had to get rid of first?" The hint of a smile touched his mouth. "And I'm not referring to my age." He was six years older than Abby. "I was pointing out that we've been seeing each other two or three times a week and suddenly you're not so sure how you feel about me."

Abby opened, then closed her mouth. She couldn't argue with what he'd said.

"That's it, isn't it?"

"Logan." She said his name on a sigh. "I like you. You know that. Over the past year I've grown very…fond of you."

"Fond?" He spat the word at her. "One

is *fond* of cats or dogs—not men. And particularly not me."

"That was a bad choice of words," Abby agreed.

"You're not exactly sure what you feel." Logan said, almost under his breath.

Abby's fingers knotted until she could feel the pain in her hands. Logan was right; she *didn't* know. She was attracted to Tate, but she knew nothing about him. The problem was that she liked what she saw. If her feelings for Logan were what they should be after a year, she wouldn't want Tate to ask her out so badly.

"You aren't sure, are you?" Logan said again.

She hung her head so that her face was framed by her dark hair. "I don't want to hurt you," she murmured.

"You haven't." Logan's hand reached across the table and squeezed her fingers reassuringly. "Beyond anything else, we're friends and I don't want to do anything to upset that friendship because it's important to me."

"That's important to me, too," she said and offered him a feeble smile. Their eyes met as the waitress came and turned over the beige cups and filled them with coffee.

"Do you want a menu?"

Abby couldn't have eaten anything and shook her head.

"Not tonight. Thanks, anyway," Logan answered for both of them.

"I don't deserve you," Abby said after the waitress had moved to the next booth.

For the first time all night Logan's lips curved into a genuine smile. "That's something I don't want you to forget."

For a few minutes they sipped their coffee in thoughtful silence. Holding the cup with both hands, she studied him. Logan's eyes were as brown as Tate's. Funny she hadn't remembered how brown they were. Tonight the color was intense, deeper than ever. They made quite a couple; she was so emotional—and he wasn't. Abby noticed that Logan's jaw was well-defined. Tate's jaw, although different, revealed that same quality—determination. With Logan, Abby recognized there was nothing he couldn't do if he wanted. Instinctively she knew the same was true of Tate.

She sensed that there were definite similarities between Logan and Tate, and yet she was reacting to them in different ways.

It seemed unfair that a man she'd seen only a couple of times could affect her like this. If she fell madly in love with someone, it should be Logan.

"What are you thinking about?" His words broke into her troubled thoughts.

Abby shrugged. "Oh, this and that," she said vaguely.

"You didn't even add sugar to your coffee."

Abby grimaced. "No wonder it tastes so awful."

Chuckling, he handed her the sugar canister.

Pouring some onto her spoon, Abby stirred it into her coffee. Logan had a nice mouth, she reflected. She couldn't remember thinking that in a long time. She had when they'd first met, but that was nearly two years ago. She watched him for a moment, trying to figure him out. Logan was so—Abby searched for the right word—sensible. Nothing ever seemed to rattle him. There wasn't an obstacle he couldn't overcome with cool reason. For once, Abby wanted him to do something crazy and nonsensical and fun.

"Logan." She spoke softly, coaxingly. "Let's drive to Des Moines tonight."

He looked at her as if she'd lost her mind. "Des Moines, Iowa?"

"Yes. Wouldn't it be fun just to take off and drive for hours—and then turn around and come home?"

"That's not fun, that's torture. Anyway, what's the point?"

Abby pressed her lips together and nodded. She shouldn't have asked. She'd known his answer even before he spoke.

The ride home was as silent as the drive to class. The tension wasn't nearly as great, but it was still evident.

"I have the feeling you're angry," Logan said as he parked in front of her building. "I'm sorry that spending the whole night on the road doesn't appeal to me. I've got this silly need for sleep. From what I understand, it affects older people."

"I'm not angry," Abby said firmly. She felt disappointed, but not angry.

Logan's hand caressed her cheek, curving around her neck and directing her mouth to his. Abby closed her eyes, expecting the usual feather-light kiss. Instead, Logan pulled her into his arms and kissed her soundly. Deeply. Passionately. Surprised but delighted,

Abby groaned softly, liking it. Her hands slipped over his shoulders and joined at the base of his neck.

Logan had never kissed her with such intensity, such unrestrained need. His mouth moved over hers, and Abby sucked in a startled breath as pure sensation shot through her. When he released her, she sighed longingly and rested her head against his chest. Involuntarily, a picture of Tate entered her mind. This was what she'd imagined kissing *him* would be like....

"You were pretending I was Tate, weren't you?" Logan whispered against her hair.

Two

"Oh, Logan, of course I wasn't," Abby answered somewhat guiltily. She *had* thought of Tate, but she hadn't pretended Logan's kiss was Tate's.

He brushed his face along the side of her hair. Abby was certain he wanted to say something more, but he didn't, remaining silent as he climbed out of the car and walked around to her side. She smiled weakly as he offered her his hand. Logan could be such a gentleman. She was perfectly capable of getting out of a car by herself, but he always wanted to help. Abby supposed she should be grateful—but she wasn't. Those old-

fashioned virtues weren't the ones that
really mattered to her.

Lightly, he kissed her again outside her
lobby door. Letting herself in, Abby was
aware that Logan waited on the other
side until he heard her turn the lock.

After changing into her long night-
gown, Abby went into the kitchen and
poured a glass of milk. She sat at the
small round table and placed her feet on
the edge of a chair, pulling her gown
over her knees. Did she love Logan? The
answer came almost immediately. Although he'd taken offense, "fond" had
aptly described her feelings. She liked
Logan, but Tate had aroused far more
emotion during their short acquaintance.
Downing the milk, Abby turned off the
light and miserably decided to go to bed.
Dano joined her, purring loudly as he arranged himself at her feet.

Friday evening, she begged off when
Logan invited her to a movie, saying she
was tired and didn't feel well. He seemed

to accept that quite readily. And, in fact, she watched a DVD at home, by herself, and was in bed by ten, reading a new mystery novel, with Dano stretched out at her side.

Saturday afternoon, Abby arrived at the park a half-hour early, hoping Tate would be there and they'd have a chance to talk. She hadn't heard from him and wondered if he'd decided Logan had a prior claim to her affection. However, Tate didn't seem the type who'd be easily discouraged. She found him in the same spot as last week and waved happily.

"I was hoping you'd be here," she said eagerly and sat on the grass beside him, leaning her back against the massive tree trunk.

"My thoughts exactly," Tate replied, with a warm smile that elevated Abby's heart rate.

"I'm sorry about Logan," she told him, weaving her fingers through the grass.

"No need to apologize."

"But he was so rude," Abby returned, feeling guilty for being unkind. But she'd said no less to Logan himself.

Tate sent her a look of surprise. "He didn't behave any differently than I would have, had the circumstances been reversed."

"Logan doesn't own me," she said defiantly.

A smile bracketed the edges of his mouth. "That's one piece of news I'm glad to hear."

Their eyes met and he smiled. Abby could feel her bones melt. It was all she could do to smile back.

"Do you like in-line skating?"

"I love it." She hadn't skated since she was a teen at the local roller rink, but if Tate suggested they stand on their heads in the middle of the road, Abby probably would have agreed.

"Would you like to meet me here tomorrow afternoon?"

"Sure," she said without hesitating. "Here?" she repeated, sitting up.

"You *have* skated?" He gave her a worried glance.

"Oh, sure." Her voice squeaked, embarrassing her. "Tomorrow? What time?"

"Three," Tate suggested. "After that we'll go out for something to eat."

"This is sounding better all the time," Abby teased. "But be warned, I do have a healthy appetite. Logan says—" She nearly choked on the name, immediately wishing she could take it back.

"You were saying something about Logan," Tate prompted.

"Not really." She gave a light shrug, flushing involuntarily.

Mai-Ling stepped off the bus just then and walked toward them. Abby stood up. Brushing the grass from her legs, she smiled warmly at her friend.

"Why do you meet her every week?" Tate asked. The teasing light vanished from his eyes

"I do volunteer work with the World Literacy Movement. Mai-Ling can read perfectly in Chinese, but she's an American now so I'm helping her learn to read and write English."

"Have you been a volunteer long?"

"A couple of years. Why? Would you like to help? We're always looking for volunteers."

"Me?" He looked stunned and a little shocked. "Not now. I've got more than I can handle helping at the zoo."

"The zoo?" Abby shot back excitedly. "Are you a volunteer?"

"Yes," Tate said as he stood and glanced at his watch. "I'll tell you more about it tomorrow. Right now I've got to get back to work before the boss discovers why I've taken extended lunch breaks the past four Saturdays."

"I'll look forward to tomorrow," Abby murmured, thinking she'd never known anyone as compelling as Tate.

"You met the man?" Mai-Ling asked

as she came over to Abby's side and followed her gaze to the retreating male figure.

"Yes, I met him," Abby answered wistfully. "Oh, Mai-Ling, I think I'm in love!"

"Love?" Mai-Ling frowned. "The American word for love is bad."

"Bad?" Abby repeated, not comprehending.

"Yes. In English one word means many kinds of love."

Abby turned her attention from Tate to her friend and asked, "What do you mean?"

"In America, love for a husband is the same as…as love for chocolate. I heard a lady on the bus say she *loves* chocolate, then say she is in love with a new man." Mai-Ling shook her head in astonishment and disbelief. "In Chinese it is much different. Better."

"No doubt you're right," Abby said

with a bemused grin. "I guess it's all about context."

Mai-Ling ignored that. "You will see the man again?"

"Tomorrow," Abby said dreamily. Suddenly her eyes widened. Tomorrow was Sunday, and Logan would expect her to do something with him. Oh dear, this was becoming a problem. Not only hadn't she skated in years, but she was bound to have another uncomfortable confrontation with Logan. Her eager anticipation for tomorrow was quickly replaced by a sinking feeling in the pit of her stomach.

Abby spent another miserable night. She'd attempted to phone Logan and make up another excuse about not being able to get together, but he hadn't been home. She didn't feel it was right to leave a message, which struck her as cowardly. Consequently her sleep was fitful and intermittent. It wasn't as if Logan called and arranged a time each week; they had a simple understanding that Sundays were *their* day. Arrangements for most other days were more flexible. But Abby couldn't remember a week when they hadn't gotten together on a Sunday. Her sudden decision would be as readable as the morning headlines. Logan would know she was meeting Tate.

Abby's first inclination was not to be there when he arrived, but that was even more cowardly. In addition, Abby knew Logan well enough to realize that her attempts to dodge him wouldn't work. Either he'd go to the park and look for her or he'd drive to her parents' house and worry them sick.

By the time he did arrive, Abby's stomach felt as if a lead balloon had settled inside.

"Beautiful afternoon, isn't it?" Logan came over to her and slipped an arm around her waist, drawing her close to his side. "Are you feeling better?" he asked in a concerned voice. So often in the past year, Abby had longed for him to hold her like this. Now when he did, she wanted to scream with frustration.

"Yes, I'm...okay."

"What would you like to do?" he asked, nuzzling her neck and holding her close.

"Logan." Abby hesitated, and cleared her throat, feeling guilty. "I've got other plans this afternoon." Her voice didn't even sound like her own as she squeezed her eyes shut, afraid to meet his hard gaze.

A grimness stole into his eyes as his hand tightened. "You're seeing Tate, aren't you?"

Abby caught her breath at the ferocity of his tone. "Of course not!" She couldn't look at him. For the first time in their relationship, Abby was blatantly lying to Logan. No wonder she was experiencing this terrible guilt. For one crazy minute, Abby felt like bursting into tears and running out of the apartment.

"Tell me what you're doing then," he demanded.

Abby swallowed at the painful lump in her throat. "Last week you cut our time together short," she said. "I didn't ask where you were going. I don't feel it's too much to expect the same courtesy."

Logan's grip on her waist slackened, but he didn't release her. "What about later? Couldn't we meet for dinner? There's something I wanted to discuss."

"I can't," she said quickly. Too quickly. Telltale color warmed her face.

Logan studied her for a long moment, then dropped his arm. She should've been glad. Instead she felt chilled and suddenly bereft.

"Let me know when you're free." His words were cold as he moved toward the door.

"Logan," Abby called out to him desperately. "Don't be angry. Please."

When he paused and turned around, his eyes flickered over her. She couldn't quite read his expression but she knew it wasn't flattering. Wordlessly, he turned again and left.

Abby wanted to crawl into a hole, curl up and die. Logan deserved so much better than this. Any number of women would call her a fool—and they'd be right.

Dressed in white linen shorts and a red cotton shirt, Abby studied her reflection in the full-length mirror on the back of the bedroom door. Her hair hung in a long ponytail, practical for skating, she figured. Makeup did little to disguise the doubt and unhappiness in her eyes. With a jagged breath, Abby tied the sleeves of a sweater around her neck and headed out the door.

Tate was standing by the elm tree waiting for her. He was casually dressed in jeans and a V-neck sweater that hinted at curly chest hair. Even across the park, Abby recognized the quiet authority of the man. His virile look attracted the attention of other women in the vicinity, but Tate didn't seem to notice.

He started walking toward her, his smile approving as he surveyed her long legs.

"You look like you've lost your best friend," Tate said as he slid a casual arm around her shoulder.

Abby winced; his comment might be truer than he knew.

"Problem?" he asked.

"Not really." Her voice quavered, but she managed to give him a broad smile. "I'm hoping we can rent skates. I don't have a pair."

"We can."

It didn't take long for Tate's infectious good mood to brighten Abby's spirits. Soon she was laughing at her bungling attempts to skate. A concrete pathway was very different from the smooth, polished surface of the rink. Either that, or it'd been longer than she realized since her last time on skates.

Tate tucked a hand around her hip as his movements guided hers.

"You're doing great." His eyes were smiling as he relaxed his grasp.

Laughing, Abby looked away from the pathway to answer him when her skate hit a rut and she tumbled forward, wildly thrashing her arms in an effort to remain upright. She would have fallen if Tate hadn't still been holding her. His hand tightened, bringing her closer. She faltered a bit from the effect of his nearness.

"I'm a natural," she said with a grin.

"A natural klutz," he finished for her.

They skated for two hours. When Tate suggested they stop, Abby glanced at her watch and was astonished by the time.

"Hungry?" Tate asked next.

"Famished."

The place Tate took her to was one of those relatively upscale restaurants that charged a great deal for its retro diner atmosphere, but where the reputation for excellent food was well-earned. Abby couldn't imagine Logan bringing her someplace like this. Knowing that made the outing all the more enticing.

When the waitress came, Abby ordered an avocado burger with a large stuffed baked potato and strawberry shortcake for dessert.

Tate smiled. "I'll have the same," he told the waitress, who wrote down their order and stepped away from the table.

"So you do volunteer work at the zoo?" Abby was interested in learning the details he'd promised to share with her.

"I've always loved animals," he began.

"I could tell from the way you talked to the ducks and the squirrels," Abby inserted, recalling the first time she'd seen Tate.

He acknowledged her statement with a nod. "Even as a child I'd bring home in-

jured animals—rabbits, raccoons, squirrels—and do what I could to make them
well."

"Why didn't you become a veterinar-
ian?"

Tate ignored the question. "The hardest part was setting them free once they
were well. I might have been a veterinar-
ian if things in my life had gone differently, but I'm good with cars, too."

"You're a mechanic?" Abby asked, already knowing the answer. The callused
hands told her that her guess couldn't be
far off.

"I work at Bessler's Auto Repair."

"Sure. I know it. That's across the
street from the Albertsons' store."

"That's it."

So it *had* just been a coincidence that
she'd seen Tate in the store; he worked
in the immediate vicinity.

"I've been working there since I was
seventeen," Tate added. "Jack Bessler is
thinking about retirement these days."

"What'll happen to the shop?"

"I'm hoping to buy it," Tate said as he held his fork, nervously rotating it between two fingers.

Tate was uneasy about something. He ran his fingers up and down the fork, not lifting his gaze from his silverware.

Their meal was as delicious as Abby knew it would be. Whatever had bothered Tate was soon gone and the remainder of the evening was spent talking, getting to know each other with an eagerness that was as strong as their mutual attraction. They talked nonstop for hours, sauntering lazily along the water's edge and laughing, neither of them eager to bring their time together to a close.

When Abby finally got home it was nearly midnight. She floated into the apartment on a cloud of happiness. Even as she readied for bed, she couldn't forget how wonderful the night had been. Tate was a man she could talk to, really talk to. He listened to her and seemed to understand her feelings. Logan listened, too, but Abby had the impression that he sometimes felt impatient with her. But perhaps that wasn't it at all. Maybe she was looking for ways to soothe her conscience. His reaction today still shocked her; as far as she was concerned, they hadn't made any commitment to each other beyond that of friendship. Sometimes Abby wondered if she really knew Logan.

The phone rang fifteen minutes after she was in the door.

Assuming it was Tate, Abby all but flew across the room to answer it, not bothering to check call display. "Hello," she said in a low, sultry voice.

"Abby, is that you? You don't sound right. Are you sick?"

It was Logan.

Instantly, Abby stiffened and sank into the comfort of her chair. "Logan," she said in her normal voice. "Hi. Is something wrong?" He wouldn't be phoning this late otherwise.

"Not really."

"I just got in…I mean…" She faltered as her thoughts tripped over each other. "I thought you might be in bed, so I didn't call," she finished lamely. He was obviously phoning to find out what time she got home.

Deftly Logan changed the subject to a matter of no importance, confirming Abby's suspicions. "No," he said, "I was just calling to see what time you wanted me to pick you up for class on Tuesday."

Of all the feeble excuses! "Next time I go somewhere without you, do you want me to phone in so you'll know the precise minute I get home?" she asked crisply, fighting her temper as her hand tightened around the receiver.

His soft chuckle surprised her. "I guess I wasn't very original, was I?"

"No. This isn't like you, Logan. I've never thought of you as the jealous type."

"There's a lot you don't know about me," he answered on a wry note.

"I'm beginning to realize that."

"Do you want me to pick you up for class this week, or have you…made other arrangements?"

"Of course I want you to pick me up! I wouldn't want it any other way." Abby meant that. She liked Logan. The problem was she liked Tate, too.

Logan hesitated and the silence stretched between them. Abby was sure he could hear her racing heart over the phone. But she hoped he couldn't read the confusion in her mind.

After work on Monday afternoon, instead of heading back to her apartment and Dano, Abby stopped off at her parents' house.

"Hi, Mom." She sauntered into the kitchen and kissed her mother on the cheek. "What's there to eat?" Opening the refrigerator door, Abby surveyed the contents with interest.

"Abby," her mother admonished, "what's wrong?"

"Wrong?" Abby feigned ignorance.

"Abby, I'm your mother. I know you. The only time you show up in the middle of the week is if something's bothering you."

"Honestly, aren't I allowed an unexpected visit without parental analysis?"

"Did you and Logan have a fight?" her mother persisted.

Glenna Carpenter's chestnut hair was as dark as Abby's but streaked with gray, creating an unusual color a hairdresser couldn't reproduce. Glenna was a young sixty, vivacious, outgoing and—like Abby—a doer.

"What makes you say that? Logan and I never fight." Abby chewed on a stalk of celery and closed the refrigerator. Taking the salt from the cupboard beside the stove she sprinkled some on it.

"Salt's bad for your blood pressure." Glenna took the shaker out of Abby's hand and replaced it in the cupboard. "Are you going to tell me what's wrong?" She spoke in a warning tone that Abby knew better than to disregard.

"Honest, Mom, there's nothing."

"Abby." Sapphire-blue eyes snapped with displeasure.

Abby couldn't hold back a soft laugh. Her mother had a way of saying more with one glare than some women did with a tantrum.

Holding the celery between her teeth, Abby placed both hands on the counter and pulled herself up, sitting beside the sink.

"Abby," her mother said a second time.

"It's Logan." She gave a frustrated sigh. "He's become so possessive lately."

"Well, thank goodness. I'd have thought you'd be happy." Glenna's smiling eyes revealed her approval. "I was wondering how long it would take him."

"Mother!" Abby wanted to cry. Deep in her heart, she'd known her mother would react like this. "It's too late—I've met someone else."

Glenna froze and a shocked look came over her. "Who?"

"His name is Tate Harding."

"When?"

"A couple of weeks ago."

"How old is he?"

Abby wanted to laugh at her mother's questions. She sounded as if Abby was fifteen again and asking for permission to date. "He's twenty-seven and a hardworking, respectable citizen. I don't know how to explain it, Mom, but I was instantly attracted to him. I think I'm falling in love."

"Falling in love," Glenna echoed, reheating the day's stale coffee and pouring herself a cup. Her hand shook as she lifted the mug to her mouth a couple of minutes later.

Abby knew her mother was taking her

seriously when she drank coffee, which she usually reserved for mornings. A smile tugged at Abby's mouth, but she successfully restrained it.

"I know what you must be thinking," Abby said. "You don't even have to say it because I've already chided myself a thousand times. Logan's the greatest man in the world, but Tate is—"

"The ultimate one?"

The suppressed smile came to life. "You could say that."

"Does Logan know?"

"Of all the luck, they ran into each other at my apartment last week. It would've helped if they hadn't met like that."

"I think having Logan and Tate stumble into each other was more providential than you realize," Glenna murmured with infuriating calm. "I've always liked Logan. I think he's perfect for you."

"How can you *say* that?" Abby demanded indignantly. "We aren't anything alike. We don't even enjoy the same things. Logan can be such a stuffed shirt. And you haven't even met Tate."

"No." Her mother ran the tip of one finger along the rim of her mug. "To be honest, I could never understand why Logan puts up with you. I love you, Abby, but I know your faults as well as your strengths. Apparently Logan sees the same potential in you that I do."

"I can't believe my own mother would talk to me like this." Abby spoke to the ceiling, venting her irritation. "I come to her to pour out my heart and seek her advice and end up being judged."

Glenna laughed. "I'm not judging you," she declared. "Just giving you some sound, motherly advice." An ardent light glowed from her eyes. "Logan loves you. He—"

"Mother," Abby interrupted. "How can you be so sure? If he does, which I sincerely doubt, then he's never told me."

"No, I don't imagine he has. Logan is waiting."

"Waiting?" Abby asked sarcastically. "For what? A blue moon?"

"No," Glenna said sharply and took a long, deliberate sip of her coffee, which must have tasted foul. "He's been waiting for you to grow up. You're impulsive and quick-tempered, especially when it comes to relationships. You expect him to take the lead and yet you resent him for it."

Abby gasped; she couldn't help it. Rarely had her mother spoken this candidly to her. Abby opened her mouth to deny the accusations, then closed it again. The words hurt, especially coming from her own mother, and she lowered her gaze to hide the onrush of emotional pain. Tears gathered in her eyes.

"I'm not saying these things to hurt you," Glenna continued softly.

"I know that." Abby grimaced. "You're

right. I should be more honest, but I don't want to hurt Logan."

"Then tell him what you're feeling. Stringing him along would be unkind."

"But it's hard," Abby protested, wiping her eyes. "If I told him yesterday that I was going out with Tate he would've been angry. And miserable."

"And do you suppose he wasn't? I know Logan. If you said anything to him, he'd immediately step aside until you've settled things in your own mind."

"I know," Abby breathed in frustration. "But I'm not sure I want that either."

"You mean you want to have your cake and eat it, too," Glenna said. "As the old cliché has it…"

"I never have understood that saying."

"Then maybe you'd better think about it, Abby."

"In other words you're telling me I should let Logan know how I feel about Tate."

"Yes. You can't have it both ways. You can't keep Logan hanging if you want to pursue a romance with this other man."

The seriousness of her mother's look, her words, transferred itself to Abby.

"Today," Glenna insisted. "Now, before you change your mind."

Slowly Abby nodded. She hopped down from the counter, prepared to talk to Logan. "Thanks, Mom."

Glenna Carpenter gave Abby a motherly squeeze. "I'll be thinking about you."

"You'll like Tate."

"I'm sure I will. You always did have excellent taste."

Abby's smile was tentative.

She knew Logan was working late tonight, so she drove straight to his accounting firm, which was situated half a block from her own office. Karen, his assistant, had gone home, and Abby knocked at the outer office. Almost instantly the door opened and Logan gestured her inside.

"Abby." He beamed her a warm smile. "What a nice surprise. Come in, won't you."

Abby took the leather chair opposite his desk.

"Logan." Her fingers had knotted into a tight fist in her lap. "Can we talk?"

He looked down at his watch.

"It won't take long, I promise," she added hurriedly.

Leaning against the side of his desk, he crossed his arms. "What is it, Abby? You never look this serious about anything."

"I think you have a right to know that I was with Tate Harding yesterday." Her heart was hammering wildly as she said this.

"Abby, you're as readable as a child. I was aware from the beginning who you were with," he told her. "I only wish that you'd been honest with me."

"Oh, Logan, I do apologize for that."

"Fine. It's forgotten."

How could he be so generous? So forgiving? Just when she was about to explain that she wanted to continue seeing Tate, Logan reached for her, drawing her into his embrace. As his mouth settled over hers, he drew from her a response so complete that Abby was left speechless and all the more confused. He kissed her as if he couldn't get enough of her mouth, of *her*.

"I've got a client meeting in five minutes," Logan whispered as he massaged her shoulders. "But believe me, holding you is far more appealing. Promise me you'll drop by the office again."

Then he let her go, and she sank back into the chair.

Three

Abby punched the pillow and determinedly shut her eyes. She shouldn't be having so much trouble falling asleep, she thought, fighting back a loud yawn. Ten minutes later, she wearily raised one eyelid and glared at the clock radio. Two-thirty! She groaned audibly. Logan was responsible for this. He should've taken the time to listen to her. Now she didn't know when she'd work up the courage to talk to him about Tate.

And speaking of Tate… He'd phoned after dinner and suggested going to the zoo that weekend. Abby couldn't refuse him. Now she was paying the price—

remorse and self-recrimination. Worse, it was all Logan's fault that she hadn't been able to explain the situation to him. She didn't mean to do anything behind his back. She liked both men, but the attraction she felt toward Tate was far more intense than the easy camaraderie she shared with Logan.

Bunching the pillow, Abby forced her eyes to close. She'd gone to Logan to tell him she wanted to date other men. She'd tried, really tried. What else could she do?

When the radio went off at six, Abby wanted to scream. Sleep had eluded her the entire night. The few hours she'd managed to catch wouldn't be enough to see her through the day. Her eyes burned as she tossed aside the covers and sat on the edge of the bed.

More from habit than anything, Abby brushed her teeth and dressed. Coffee didn't help. And the tall glass of orange juice tasted like tomato, but she didn't open her eyes to investigate.

Half an hour later, she let herself into the clinic. The phone was already ringing.

"Morning." Cheryl Hansen, the receptionist, smiled at Abby before answering the call.

Abby returned the friendly gesture with a weak smile of her own.

"You look like the morning after a wild and crazy night," Cheryl said as Abby hung her jacket in the room off the reception area.

"It was wild and crazy, all right," Abby said after an exaggerated yawn. "But not the way you think."

"Another late night with Logan?"

Abby's eyes widened. "No!"

"Tate then?"

"No. Unfortunately."

"I'm telling you, Ab, keeping track of your love life is getting more difficult all the time."

"I haven't got a love life," she murmured, unable to stop yawning. Covering her mouth, Abby moved to the end of the long hallway.

The day didn't get any better. By noon, she recognized that she couldn't possibly attend tonight's class with Logan. For one thing, she was too tired to concentrate on painting theory and technique. For another, as soon as he saw her troubled expression, he'd know immediately that she was deceiving him and seeing Tate again. And something she didn't need today was another confrontation with Logan. She didn't want to hurt him. But more than that—she didn't want to lie to him.

On her way back from lunch, Abby decided to call his office. Her guilt grew heavier at the pleasure in his voice.

"Abby! What's up?"

"Hi, Logan." She groaned inwardly. "I hope you don't mind me phoning you like this."

"Not at all."

"I'm not feeling well." She paused, her hand tightening around the receiver. "I was thinking that maybe it'd be best if I skipped class tonight."

"What's wrong?" His genuine concern was nearly her undoing. "You weren't well on Friday, either."

Did he really believe her excuse of Friday evening, which had been nothing but a way of avoiding him?

"You must be coming down with something," he said.

"I think so." *Like a terminal case of cowardice,* her mind shot back.

"Have you seen a doctor?"

"It isn't necessary. Not yet. But I thought I'd stay home again tonight and go to bed early," Abby mumbled, feeling more wretched every second.

"Do you need me to do anything for you?" His voice was laced with gentleness.

"No," she assured him quickly. "I'm

fine. Really. I just thought I'd nip this thing in the bud and take it easy."

"Okay. But promise me that if you need anything, you'll call."

"Oh, sure."

Abby felt even worse after making that phone call. By the time she returned to her apartment late that afternoon her excuse for not attending her class had become real. Her head was throbbing unmercifully; her throat felt dry and scratchy and her stomach was queasy.

With her fingertips pressing her temple, Abby located the aspirin in the bathroom cabinet and downed two tablets. Afterward she lay on the sofa, the phone beside her, head propped up with a soft pillow, and closed her eyes. She didn't open them when the phone rang and she scrabbled around for it blindly.

"Hello." Her reluctant voice was barely above a whisper.

"Abby, is that you?"

She breathed easier. It was her mother.

"Hi, Mom."

"What's wrong?"

"I've got a miserable headache."

"What's bothering you?"

"What makes you think anything's bothering me?" Her mother displayed none of the sympathy Logan had.

"Abby, I know you. When you get a headache it's because something's troubling you."

Breathing deeply, Abby glanced at the ceiling with wide-open eyes, unable to respond.

"Did you talk to Logan yesterday?" Her mother resumed the interrogation.

"Only for a little while. He was on his way to a meeting."

"Did you tell him you want to continue seeing Tate?"

"I didn't get the chance," Abby said more aggressively than she'd intended. "Mom, I tried, but he didn't have time to listen. Then Tate phoned me and asked me out this weekend and…I said yes."

"Does Logan know?"

"Not yet," she mumbled.

"And you've got a whopper of a headache?"

"Yes." The word trembled on her lips.

"Abby." Her mother's voice took on the tone Abby knew all too well. "You've *got* to talk to Logan."

"I will."

"Your headache won't go away until you do."

"I know."

Dano strolled into the room and leaped onto the sofa, settling in Abby's lap. Grateful to have one friend left in the world, Abby stroked her cat.

It took her at least twenty minutes to work up enough fortitude to call Logan's home number. His phone rang six times, and Abby sighed, not leaving a message. She assumed he'd gone to class on his own, that he was on his way, so she didn't bother trying his cell. She'd talk to him tomorrow.

She closed her eyes again, wondering how—if—she could balance her intense attraction to Tate with her feelings of friendship for Logan. Friendship that sometimes hinted at more. His ardent kiss yesterday had taken her by surprise. But she *had* to tell him about Tate....

The apartment buzzer woke Abby an hour later. She sat up and rubbed the stiff muscles of her neck. Dano remained on her lap and meowed angrily when she stood, forcing the cat to leap to the floor.

"Yes?" she said into the speaker.

"It's Logan."

Abby buzzed him in. Her hand was shaking visibly as she unlocked the door. "Hi," she said in a high-pitched voice.

Logan stepped inside. "How are you feeling?"

"I don't know." She yawned, stretching her arms. "Better, I guess." Her attention was drawn to a white sack Logan was holding. "What's that?"

A crooked smile slanted his mouth.

"Chicken soup. I picked some up at the deli." He handed her the bag. "I want to make sure you're well enough for the game tomorrow night."

Abby's head shot up. "Game? What game?"

"I wondered if you'd forgotten. We signed up a couple of weeks ago for the softball team. Remember?"

This was the second summer they were playing in the office league. With her recent worries, softball had completely slipped Abby's mind. "Oh, *that* game." Abby wanted to groan. She'd *never* be able to avoid Logan. Too many activities linked them together—work, classes and now softball.

She took the soup into the kitchen, removing the large plastic cup from the sack. The aroma of chicken and noodles wafted through the small room. Logan followed her in and slipped his arms around her waist from behind. His chin rested on her head as he spoke. "I woke you up, didn't I?"

She nodded, resisting the urge to turn and slip her arms around his waist and bury her face in his chest. "But it's probably a good thing you did. I've gotten a crick in my neck sleeping on the couch with Dano on my lap."

Logan's breath stirred the hair at the top of her head. The secure feeling of his arms holding her close was enough to bring tears to her eyes.

"Logan." She breathed his name in a husky murmur. "Why are you so good to me?"

He turned her to face him. "I would've thought you'd have figured it out by now," he said as he slowly lowered his mouth to hers.

A sweetness flooded Abby at the tender possession of his mouth. She wanted to cry and beg him *not* to love her. Not yet. Not until she was sure of her feelings. But the gentle caress of his lips prevented the words from ever forming. Her hands moved up his shirt and over his shoulders, reveling in his strength.

His hands, at the small of her back, arched her closer as he inhaled deeply. "I've got to go or I'll be late for class. Will you be all right?"

Speaking was impossible and it was almost more than Abby could do to simply nod her head.

He straightened, relaxing his grip. "Take care of yourself," he said as his eyes smiled lovingly into hers.

Again it was all Abby could do to nod.

"I'll pick you up tomorrow at six-thirty, if you're up to it. We can grab a bite to eat after the game."

"Okay," she managed shakily and walked him to the door. "Thanks for the soup."

Logan smiled. "I've got to take care of the team's first-base player, don't I?" His mouth brushed hers and he was gone.

Leaning against the door, Abby looked

around her grimly. If she felt guilty before, she felt wretched now.

Shoving the baseball cap down on her long brown hair, which she'd tied back in a loose ponytail, Abby couldn't stifle a sense of excitement. She did enjoy softball. And Logan was right—she was the best first-base player the team was likely to find. Not to mention her hitting ability.

Logan wasn't as good a player but enjoyed himself as much as she did. He just didn't have the same competitive edge. More than once he'd been responsible for an error. But no one seemed to mind and Abby didn't let it bother her.

As usual he was punctual when he came to pick her up. "Hi. I can see you're feeling better."

"Much better."

The game was scheduled to be played in Diamond Lake Park, and Abby was half-afraid Tate would stumble across them. She wasn't sure how often he went into the park and— She reined in her worries. There was no reason to assume he'd show up or that he'd even recognize her.

Most of the team had arrived by the time Abby and Logan sauntered onto the field. The Jack and Jill Softball League was recreational. Of all their team members, Abby was the one who took the game most seriously. The team positions alternated between men and women. Since Abby played first base, a man was at second. Logan was in the outfield.

The team they were playing was from a local church that Abby remembered having beaten last summer.

Dick Snyder was their office team's coach and strategist. "Hope that arm's as good as last year," Dick said to Abby, who beamed at him. It was gratifying to be appreciated.

After a few warm-up exercises and practice pitches, their team left the field. Logan was up at bat first. Abby cringed at the stiff way he held himself. He wasn't a natural athlete, despite his biking prowess.

"Logan," she shouted encouragingly, "flex your knees."

He did as she suggested and swung at the next pitch. The ground ball skidded past the shortstop and Logan was safe on first.

Abby breathed easier and sent him a triumphant smile.

Patty Martin was up at bat next. Abby took one look at the shy, awkward young woman and knew she'd be an immediate out. Patty was new to the team this year, and Abby hoped she'd stick with it.

"Come on, Patty," she called out, hoping to instill some confidence, "you can do it!"

Patty held the bat clumsily and bit her lip as she glared straight ahead at the pitcher. She swung at the first three balls and missed each one.

Dick pulled Patty aside and gave her a pep talk before she took her place on the bench.

Abby hurried over to Patty and patted her knee. "I'm glad you decided to play with us." She meant that honestly. She suspected Patty could do with some friends.

"But I'm terrible." Patty stared at her clenched hands and Abby noticed how white her knuckles were.

"You'll improve," Abby said with more certainty than she felt. "Everyone has to learn, and believe me, every one of us strikes out. Don't worry about it."

By the time Abby was up to bat, there were two outs and Logan was still at first. Her standup double and a home run by the hitter following her made the score 3-0.

It remained the same until the bottom of the eighth. Logan was playing the outfield when a high fly ball went over his head. He scrambled to retrieve it.

Frantically jumping up and down at first base, Abby screamed, "Throw the ball to second! Second." She watched in horror as Logan turned and faced third base. "Second!" she yelled angrily.

The woman on third base missed the catch, and the batter went on to make it home, giving his team their first run.

Abby threw her glove down and, with her hands placed defiantly on her hips, stormed into the outfield and up to Logan. "I told you to throw the ball to second."

He gave her a mildly sheepish look. "Sorry, Abby. All your hysterics confused me."

Groaning, Abby returned to her position.

They won the game 3-1 and afterward gathered at the local restaurant for pizza and pitchers of beer.

"You're really good," Patty said, sitting beside Abby.

"Thanks," she said, smiling into her

beer. "I was on the high-school team for three years, so I had lots of practice."

"I don't know if I'll ever learn."

"Sure you will," Logan insisted. "Besides, we need you. Didn't you notice we'd be one woman short if it wasn't for you?"

Abby hadn't noticed that, but was pleased Logan had brought it up. This quality of making people feel important had drawn Abby to him on their first date.

"I'm awful, but I really like playing. And it gives me a chance to know all of you better," Patty added shyly.

"We like having you," Abby confirmed. "And you *will* improve." Patty seemed to want the reassurance that she was needed and appreciated, and Abby didn't mind echoing Logan's words.

They ate their pizzas and joked while making plans for the game the following Wednesday evening.

Dick Snyder and his wife gave Patty a

ride home. Patty hesitated in the parking
lot. "Bye, Abby. Bye, Logan," she said
timidly. "I'll see you soon."

Abby smiled secretly to herself. Patty
was attracted to Logan. She'd praised his
skill several times that evening. Abby
didn't blame her. Logan was wonderful. True, he wasn't going to be joining
the Minnesota Twins any year soon—or
ever. But he'd made it to base every time
he was up at bat.

Logan dropped Abby off at her apartment, but didn't accept her invitation to
come in for a glass of iced tea. To be
honest, Abby was grateful. She didn't
know how much longer she could hide
from Logan that she was continuing
to see Tate. And she refused to lie if
he asked her. She planned to tell him
soon...as soon as an appropriate opportunity presented itself.

The remainder of the week went
smoothly. She didn't talk to Logan,
which made things easier. Abby realized

that Sunday afternoon with him would be difficult after spending Saturday with Tate, but she decided to worry about it then.

She woke Saturday morning with a sense of expectation. Tate was taking the afternoon off and meeting her in the park after she'd finished tutoring Mai-Ling. From there they were driving out to Apple Valley and the Minnesota Zoo where he did volunteer work.

She wore a pale pink linen summer dress and had woven her long brown hair into a French braid. A glance in the mirror revealed that she looked her best.

Mai-Ling met her and smiled knowingly. "You and Tate are seeing each other today?"

"We're going to the zoo."

"The animal place, right?"

"Right."

Abby's attention drifted while Mai-Ling did her lesson. The woman's ability was increasing with every meeting.

Judging by the homework Mai-Ling brought for Abby to examine, the young woman wouldn't be needing her much longer.

They'd finished their lesson and were laughing when Abby looked up and saw Tate strolling across the lawn toward her.

Again she was struck by the sight of this ruggedly appealing male. He was dressed in jeans, a tight-fitting T-shirt and cowboy boots.

His rich brown eyes seemed to burn into hers. "Hello, Abby." He greeted Mai-Ling, but his eyes left Abby's only for a second.

"I'll catch my bus," said Mai-Ling, excusing herself, but Abby barely noticed.

"You're looking gorgeous today," Tate commented, taking her hand in his.

A tingling sensation shot up her arm at his touch. Her nerves felt taut just from standing beside him. Abby couldn't help wondering what kissing Tate would be like. Probably the closest thing to heaven this side of earth.

"You seem deep in thought."

Abby smiled up at him. "Sorry. I guess I was."

They chatted easily as Tate drove toward Apple Valley. Abby learned that he'd been a volunteer for three years, working at the zoo as many as two days a week.

"What animals do you care for?"

Tate answered her without taking his eyes off the road. "Most recently I've been working with a llama for the Family Farm, but I also do a lot of work with birds. In fact, I've been asked to assist in the bird show."

"Will you?" Abby remembered seeing Tate that first day with the ducks....

"Yes."

"What other kinds of things do you do?"

Tate's returning smile was quick. "Nothing that glamorous. I help at feeding time and I clean the cages. Sometimes I groom and exercise the animals."

"What are you doing with the llama?"

"Mostly I've been working to familiarize him with people. We'd like Larry to join his brother in giving children rides."

Tate parked the car and came around to her side to open the passenger door. He kept her hand tucked in his as he led the way to the entrance.

"You love it here, don't you?" Abby asked as they cleared the gates.

"I do. The zoo gives us a rare opportunity to discover nature and our relationship to other living things. We have a responsibility to protect animals, as well as their habitats. Zoos, good zoos like this, are part of that." A glint of laughter flashed in his eyes as he turned toward her. "I didn't know I could be so profound."

Someone called out to Tate, and Abby watched him respond with a brief wave.

"Where would you like to start?"

The zoo was divided into five regions and Abby chose Tropics Trail, an indoor oasis of plants and animals from Asia.

As they walked, Tate explained what they were seeing, regaling her with fascinating bits of information. She'd been to the zoo before, but she'd never had such a knowledgeable guide.

Three hours later, it was closing time.

"Promise you'll bring me again," Abby begged, her eyes held by Tate's with mesmerizing ease.

"I promise," he whispered as he led her toward his car.

The way he said it made her feel weak in the knees, made her forget everything and everyone else. She lapsed into a dreamy silence on the drive home.

Tate drove back to Minneapolis and they stopped at a Mexican restaurant near Diamond Lake Park. Abby had passed it on several occasions but never eaten there.

A young Hispanic waitress smiled at them and led them to a table.

Tate spoke to the woman in Spanish. She nodded her head and turned around.

"What did you ask?" Abby whispered.

"I wanted to know if we could eat outside. You don't mind, do you? The evening is lovely."

"No, that sounds great." But she did mind. Because it immediately occurred to her that Logan might drive past and see her eating there with Tate. Abby managed to squelch her worries as she sat down at a table on the patio and opened her menu. She studied its contents, but her appetite had unexpectedly disappeared.

"You've got that thoughtful look again," Tate remarked. "Is everything okay, Abby?"

"Oh, sure," she said.

Abby decided what she'd order and took the opportunity to watch Tate as he reviewed the menu. His brow was creased, his eyes narrowed in concentration. When he happened to glance up and found her looking at him he set the menu aside.

An awkwardness followed. It continued until the waitress finally stopped at their table. Abby ordered cheese enchiladas and a margarita; Tate echoed her choice but asked for a Corona beer. "I had a good time today," Abby said in an attempt to breach the silence after the waitress left.

"I did, too." Tate sounded stiff, as if he suddenly felt uneasy.

"Is something wrong?" Abby asked after another silence.

It could have been Abby's imagination, but she sensed that Tate was struggling within himself.

"Tate?" she prompted.

He leaned forward and pinched the bridge of his nose before exhaling loudly. "No…nothing."

Long after he'd dropped her off at the

apartment, Abby couldn't shake the sensation that something was troubling him. Twice he'd seemed about to speak, but both times he'd stopped himself.

Abby's thoughts were heavy as she drifted into sleep. Tomorrow she'd be spending the afternoon with Logan. She had to tell him she'd decided to see Tate; delaying it any longer was a grave disservice to them both—to Logan *and* to Tate.

Sunday afternoon, Logan sat on the sofa beside Abby and reached for her hand. She had to force herself not to snatch it away. So often in the past Abby had wanted Logan to be more demonstrative. And now that he was, it caused such turmoil inside her that she wanted to cry.

"You're looking pale, Abby. Are you sure you're feeling all right?" he asked her, his voice concerned.

"Logan, I've got to talk to you," she blurted out miserably. "I need to—"

"What you need is to get out of this stuffy apartment." He stood up, bringing her with him. Slipping an arm around her waist, Logan directed her out of the apartment and to his car.

Abby didn't have time to protest as he opened the door. She climbed inside and he leaned across to fasten her seat belt.

"Where are we going?" she asked, confused and unhappy as he backed out of the parking area.

"For a drive."

"I don't want to go for a drive."

Logan glanced away from the road long enough to narrow his eyes slightly at her. "Abby, what is it? You look like you're about to cry."

"I am." She swallowed convulsively and bit her bottom lip. "I want to go back to the apartment."

Logan pulled over and cut the engine.

"Abby, what's wrong?" he asked solicitously.

Abby got out and leaned against the side of the car. The blood was pounding wildly in her ears. She hugged her waist with both arms.

"Abby?" he prompted softly as he joined her.

"I tried to tell you on Monday evening," she said. "I even went to your office, but you had some stupid meeting."

He didn't argue with her. "Is this about Tate?"

"Yes!" she shouted. "I went to the zoo with him yesterday. All week I've felt guilty because I know you don't want me to see anyone except you."

Abby chanced a look at him. He displayed no emotion, his eyes dark and unreadable. "Do you want to continue seeing him?" he asked carefully.

"I like Tate. I've liked him from the time we met," Abby admitted in a low whisper. "I don't know him all that well, but—"

"You want to get to know him better?" His eyes seemed to draw her toward him like a magnet.

"Yes," she whispered, gazing up at him.

"Then you should," he said evenly.

"Oh, Logan," she breathed. "I was hoping you'd understand."

"I do, Abby." He placed his hands deep inside his pants pockets and walked around the car, opening the passenger door.

"Where are we going?"

He looked mildly surprised. "I'm taking you home."

The smile that touched the corners of his mouth didn't reach his eyes. "Abby, if you're seeing Tate, you won't be seeing me."

Four

Shocked, Abby stared at him, and her voice trembled slightly. "What do you mean?"

"Isn't it obvious?" Logan turned toward her. His eyes had darkened and grown more intense. There was an almost imperceptible movement along his jaw. "Remind me. How long have we been dating?" he asked, but his voice revealed nothing.

"You know how long we've been dating. About a year now. What's that got to do with anything?"

Logan frowned. "If you don't know how you feel about me in that length of time, then I can't see continuing a relationship."

Abby clenched her fist, feeling impotent anger well up within her. "You're trying to blackmail me, aren't you?"

"Blackmail you?" Logan snapped. He paused and breathed in deeply. "No, Abby, that isn't my intention."

"But you're saying that if I go out with Tate, then I can't see you," she returned with a short, bitter laugh. "You're not being fair. I like you both. You're wonderful, Logan, but...but so is Tate."

"Then decide. Which one of us do you want?"

Logan made it sound so simple. "I can't." She inhaled a shaky breath and raked a weary hand through her hair. "It's not that easy."

"Do you want Tate and me to slug it out? Is that it? Winner takes the spoils?"

"No!" she cried, shocked and angry.

"You've got the wrong man if you think I'll do that."

Tears spilled from Abby's eyes. "That's not what I want, and you know it."

"Then what *do* you want?" The low question was harsh.

"Time. I…I need to sort through my feelings. When did it become a crime to feel uncertain? I barely know Tate—"

"Time," Logan interrupted, but the anger in his tone didn't seem directed at her. "That's exactly what I'm giving you. Take as long as you need. When you've decided what you feel, let me know."

"But you won't see me?"

"Seeing you will be unavoidable. Our offices are half a block apart—and we have the softball team."

"Classes?"

"No. There's no need for us to go together or to meet each other there."

Tilting her chin downward, Abby swiped at her tears, trying to quell the rush of hurt. Logan could remove her from his life so effortlessly. His apparent indifference pierced her heart.

Without a word, he drove her back to the apartment building and parked, but didn't shut off the engine.

"Before you go," Abby said, her voice quavering, "would you hold me? Just once?"

Logan's hand tightened on the steering wheel until his knuckles were strained and white. "Do you want a comparison? Is that it?" he asked in a cold, stiff voice.

"No, that wasn't what I wanted." She reached for the door handle. "I'm sorry I asked."

Logan didn't move. They drew each breath in unison. Unflinching, their eyes held each other until Logan, his clenched jaw, hard and proud, became a watery blur and Abby lowered her gaze.

"Call me, Abby. But only when you're sure." The words were meant as a dismissal and the minute she was out of his car, he drove away.

Abby's knees felt so weak, she sat down as soon as she got inside her apartment. She was stunned. She'd expected Logan to be angry, but she'd never expected this—that he'd refuse to see her again. She'd only tried to be fair. Hurting Logan, or Tate for that matter, was the last thing she wanted. But how could she possibly know what she felt toward Tate? Everything was still so new. As she'd told Logan, they barely knew each other. They hadn't so much as kissed. But she and Logan were supposed to be friends....

She moped around the house for a couple of hours, then thought she'd pay her parents a visit. Her mother would be as shocked at Logan's reaction as she'd been. Abby needed reassurance that she'd done the right thing, especially since nothing had worked out as she'd hoped.

The short drive to her parents' house was accomplished in a matter of minutes. But there was no response to her knock; her parents appeared to be out.

Belatedly, Abby recalled her mother saying that they were going camping that weekend.

Abby slumped on the front steps, feeling enervated and depressed. Eventually she returned to her car, without any clear idea of where she should go or what she should do.

Never had a Sunday been so dull. Abby drove around for a time, picked up a hamburger at a drive-in and washed her car. Without Logan, the day seemed empty.

Lying in bed that night, Dano at her feet, Abby closed her eyes. If she'd missed Logan, he must have felt that same sense of loss. This could work both ways. Logan would soon discover how much of a gap she'd left in *his* life.

The phone rang Monday evening and Abby glanced at it anxiously. It had to be Logan, she thought hopefully. Who else would be calling? She didn't recognize the number, so maybe he had a new cell, she told herself.

"Hello," she said cheerfully. If it *was* Logan, she didn't want him to get the impression that she was pining away for him.

"Abby, it's Tate."

Tate. An unreasonable sense of disappointment filled her. What was the matter with her? This whole mess had come about because she wanted to be with Tate.

"How about a movie Friday evening?"

"I'd like that." She exhaled softly.

"You don't sound like yourself. Is something wrong?"

"No," she denied quickly. "What movie would you like to see?"

They spoke for a few more minutes and Abby managed to steer the conversation away from herself. For those few minutes, Tate helped her forget how miserable she was, but the feelings of loss and frustration returned the moment she hung up.

Tuesday evening, Abby waited outside the community center hoping to see Logan before class. She planned to give him a regal stare that would show how content she was without him. Naturally, if he gave any hint of his own unhappiness, she might succumb and speak to him. But either he'd arrived before her or after she'd gone into the building, because Abby didn't catch a glimpse of him anywhere. Maybe he'd even skipped class, but she doubted that. Logan loved chess.

The painting class remained a blur in her mind as she hurried out the door to the café across the street. She'd met Logan there after every class so far. He'd come; Abby was convinced of it. She pictured how their eyes would meet and intuitively they'd know that being apart like this was wrong for them. Logan would walk to her table, slip in beside her and take her hand. Everything would be there in his eyes for her to read.

The waitress gave Abby a surprised glance and asked if she was sitting alone tonight as she handed her the menu. Dejectedly Abby acknowledged that she was alone...at least for now.

When Logan entered the café, Abby straightened, her heart racing. He looked as good as he always did. What she didn't see was any outward sign of unhappiness...or relief at her presence. But, she reminded herself, Logan wasn't one to display his emotions openly. Their eyes met and he gave her an abrupt nod before sliding into a booth on the opposite side of the room.

So much for daydreams, Abby mused. Well, fine, he could sit there all night, but she refused to budge. Logan would have to come to her. Determinedly she studied the menu, pretending indifference. When she couldn't stand it any longer, she glanced at him from the corner of her eye. He now shared his booth with two other guys and was chatting easily with his friends. Abby's heart sank.

"I'm telling you, Mother," Abby said the next afternoon in her mother's kitchen. "He's blown this whole thing out of proportion."

"What makes you say that?" Glenna Carpenter closed the oven door and set the meat loaf on top of the stove.

"Logan isn't even talking to me."

"It doesn't seem like there's been much opportunity. But I wouldn't worry. He will tonight at the game."

"What makes you so sure of that?" Abby hopped down from her position on the countertop.

Glenna straightened and wiped her hands on her ever-present terry cloth apron. "Things have a way of working out for the best, Abby," she continued nonchalantly.

"Mom, you've been telling me that all my life and I've yet to see it happen."

Glenna chuckled, slowly shaking her head. "It happens every day of our lives. Just look around." Deftly she turned the meat loaf onto a platter. "By the way, didn't you say your game's at six o'clock?"

Abby nodded and glanced at her watch, surprised that the time had passed so quickly. "Gotta rush. Bye, Mom." She gave her mother a peck on the cheek. "Wish me well."

"With Logan or the game?" Teasing blue eyes so like her own twinkled merrily.

"Both!" Abby laughed and was out the door.

Glenna followed her to the porch, and Abby felt her mother's sober gaze as she hurried down the front steps and to her car.

Almost everyone was on the field warming up when Abby got there. Im-

Logan on the bench during the game and how she made excuses to be near him at every opportunity.

"You're coming for pizza, aren't you?" Dick asked Abby for the second time.

Abby wanted to go. The get-togethers after the game were often more fun than the game itself. But she couldn't bear the curious stares that were sure to follow when Logan sat next to Patty and started flirting with her.

"Not tonight," Abby responded, opening her eyes wide to give Dick a look of false candor. "I've got other plans." Abby noticed the way Logan's mouth curved in a mirthless smile. He'd heard that and come to his own conclusions. Good!

Abby regretted her hasty refusal later. The apartment was hot and muggy. Even Dano, her temperamental cat, didn't want to spend time with her.

After a cool shower, Abby fixed a meal of scrambled eggs, toast and a chocolate

mediately her gaze sought out Logan. He was in the outfield pitching to another of the male players. Abby tried to suppress the emotion that charged through her. Who would've believed she'd feel so lost and unhappy without Logan? If he saw that Abby had arrived, he gave no indication.

"Hi, Abby," Patty called, waving from the bench.

Abby smiled absently. "Hi."

"Wait until you see me bat." Patty beamed happily, pretending to swing at an imaginary pitch. Then, placing her hand over her eyes as the fantasy ball flew into left field, she added, "I think I'll be up for an award by the end of the season."

"Good." Abby was preoccupied as she stared out at Logan. He looked so attractive. So vital. Couldn't he have the decency to develop some lines at his eyes or a few gray hairs? He *had* to be suffering. She was, although it wasn't what she'd wanted or expected.

"Logan took me to see the Twins play on Monday night and he gave me a few pointers afterward," Patty continued.

Abby couldn't believe what she was hearing. *A few pointers? I'll just bet he did!* Logan and Patty?

The shock must have shown in her eyes because Patty added hurriedly, "You don't mind, do you? When Logan phoned, I asked him about the two of you and he said you'd both decided to start seeing other people."

"No, I don't mind," Abby returned flippantly, remembering her impression last week—that Patty had a crush on him. "Why should I?"

"I...I just wanted to be sure."

If Patty thought she'd get an award for baseball, Abby was sure someone should nominate *her* for an Oscar. By the end of the game her face hurt from her permanent smile. She laughed, cheered, joked

and tried to suggest that she hadn't a care in the world. At bat she was dynamite. Her pain was readily transferred to her swing and she didn't hit anything less than a double and got two home runs.

Once, Logan had patted her affectionately on the back to congratulate her, Abby had shot him an angry glare. It'd taken him only one day. *One day* to ask Patty out. That hurt.

"Abby?" Logan's dark brows rose questioningly. "What's wrong?"

"Wrong?" Although she gave him a blank look, she realized her face must have divulged her feelings. "What could possibly be wrong? By the way, Tate said hello. He wanted to be here tonight, but something came up." Abby knew her lie was childish, but she couldn't help her reaction.

She didn't speak to him again.

Gathering the equipment after the game, Abby tried not to remember the way Patty had positioned herself next to

bar. She wasn't the least bit hungry, but eating was at least a distraction.

She couldn't concentrate on her newest suspense novel, so she sat on the sofa and turned on the TV. A rerun of an old situation comedy helped block out the image of Patty in Logan's arms. Abby didn't doubt that Logan had kissed Patty. The bright, happy look in her eyes had said as much.

Uncrossing her legs, Abby released a bitter sigh. She shouldn't care if Logan kissed a hundred women. But she did. It bothered her immensely—regardless of her own hopes and fantasies about Tate. She recognized how irrational she was being, and her confusion only increased.

With the television blaring to drown out the echo of Patty's telling her about the fun she'd had with Logan, Abby reached for the chocolate bar and peeled off the wrapper. The sweet flavor wouldn't ease the discomfort in her stomach, because Abby knew it wasn't chocolate she wanted, it was Logan. Feeling wretched again, she set the candy bar aside and leaned her head back, closing her eyes.

By Friday evening, Abby was convinced all the contradictory feelings she had about Logan could be summed up in one sentence: The grass is always greener on the other side of the fence. It was another of those clichés her mother seemed so fond of and spouted on a regular basis. She was surprised Glenna hadn't dragged this one into their conversations about Logan and Tate. The idea of getting involved with Tate had been appealing when she was seeing Logan steadily. It stood to reason that the reverse was also true—that Logan would miss her and lose interest in Patty. At least that was what Abby told herself repeatedly as she dressed for her date.

With her long brown hair a frame around her oval face, she put on more makeup than usual. With a secret little smile she applied an extra dab of perfume. Tate wouldn't know what hit him! The summer dress was one of her best— a pale blue sheath that could be dressed up or down, so she was as comfortable wearing it to a movie as she would be to a formal dinner.

When Tate arrived, he had on a pair of cords and a cotton shirt, open at the neck, sleeves rolled up. It was undeniably a sexy look.

"You're stunning," he said appreciatively, kissing her lightly on the cheek.

"Thank you." Abby couldn't restrain her disappointment. He'd looked at her the way one would a sister and his kiss wasn't that of a lover—or someone who intended to be a lover.

Still, they joked easily as they waited in line for the latest blockbuster action movie and Abby was struck by their camaraderie. It didn't take her long to realize that their relationship wasn't hot and fiery, sparked by mutual attraction. Instead, it was...friendly. Warm. Almost lacking in imagination. Ironically, that had been exactly her complaint about Logan....

Tate bought a huge bucket of popcorn, which they shared in the darkened theater. But Abby noted that he appeared restless, often shifting his position, crossing and uncrossing his legs. Once, when he assumed she wasn't watching, he laid his head against the back of the seat and closed his eyes. Was Tate in pain? she wondered.

Abby's attention drifted from the movie. "Tate," she whispered. "Are you okay?"

He immediately opened his eyes. "Of course. Why?"

Rather than refer to his restlessness, she simply shook her head and pretended an interest in the screen.

When they'd finished the popcorn, Tate reached for her hand. But Abby noted that it felt tense. If she didn't know better, she'd swear he was nervous. But Abby couldn't imagine what possible reason Tate would have to be nervous around her.

The evening was hot and close when they emerged from the theater.

"Are you hungry?" Tate asked, taking her hand, and again, Abby was struck by how unnaturally tense he seemed.

"For something cold and sinful," she answered with a teasing smile.

"Beer?"

"No," Abby said with a laugh. "Ice cream."

Tate laughed, too, and hand in hand they strolled toward the downtown area where Tate assured her he knew of an old-fashioned ice-cream place. The Swanson Parlor was decorated in pink— pink walls, pink chairs, pink linen table- cloths and pink-dressed waitresses.

Abby decided quickly on a banana split and mentioned it to Tate.

"That does sound good. I'll have one, too."

Abby shut her menu and set it aside. This was the third time they'd gone for something to eat, and each time Tate had ordered the same thing she did. He didn't seem insecure. But maybe she was being oversensitive. Besides, it didn't make any difference.

Their rapport made conversation comfortable and lighthearted. They talked about the movie and other films they'd both seen. Abby discussed some of her favorite mystery novels and Tate described animal behavior he'd witnessed. But several times Abby noted that his laughter was forced. His gaze would become intent and his sudden seriousness would throw the conversation off stride.

"I love Minneapolis," Abby said as they left the ice-cream parlor. "It's such a livable city."

"I agree," Tate commented. "Do you want to go for a walk?"

"Yes, let's." Abby tucked her hand in the crook of his elbow.

Tate looked at her and smiled, but again Abby noted the sober look in his eyes. "I was born in California," he began.

"What's it like there?" Abby had been to New York but she'd never visited the West Coast.

"I don't remember much. My family moved to New Mexico when I was six."

"Hot, I'll bet," Abby said.

"It's funny, the kinds of things you remember. I don't recall what the weather was like. But I have a very clear memory of my first-grade teacher in Alburquerque, Ms. Grimes. She was pretty and really tall." Tate chuckled. "But I suppose all teachers are tall to a six-year-old. We moved again in the middle of that year."

"You seem to have moved around quite a bit," Abby said, wondering why Tate had started talking about himself so freely. Although they had talked about a number of different subjects, she knew little about his personal life.

"We moved five times in as many years," Tate continued. "We had no choice, really. My dad couldn't hold down a job, and every time he lost one we'd pack up and move, seeking another start, another escape." Tate's face hardened. "We came to Minneapolis when I was in the eighth grade."

"Did your father finally find his niche in life?" Abby sensed that Tate was revealing something he rarely shared with anyone. She felt honored, but surprised. Their relationship was promising in some ways and disappointing in others, but the fact that he trusted her with his pain, his difficult past, meant a lot. She wondered why he'd chosen her as a confidante.

"No, Dad died before he ever found what he was looking for." There was no disguising the anguish in his voice. "My feelings for my father are as confused now as they were then." He turned toward Abby, his expression solemn. "I hated him and I loved him."

"Did your life change after he was gone?" Abby's question was practically a whisper, respecting the deep emotion in Tate's eyes.

"Yes and no. A couple of years later, I dropped out of school and got a job as a mechanic. My dad taught me a lot, enough to persuade Jack Bessler to hire me."

"And you've been there ever since?"

His mouth quirked at one corner. "Ever since."

"You didn't graduate from high school then, did you?"

"No."

That sadness was back in his voice. "And you resent that?" Abby asked softly.

"I may have for a time, but I never fit in a regular classroom. I guess in some ways I'm a lot like my dad. Restless and insecure. But I'm much more content working at the garage than I ever was in a classroom."

"You've worked there for years now," Abby said, contradicting his assessment of himself. "How can you say you're restless?"

He didn't acknowledge her question. "There's a chance I could buy the business. Jack's ready to retire and wants out from under the worry."

"That's what you really want, isn't it, Tate?"

"The business is more than I ever thought I'd have."

"But something's stopping you?" Abby could sense this more from his tension than from what he said.

"Yes." The stark emotion in his voice startled her.

"Are you worried about not having graduated from high school? Because, Tate, you can now. There's a program at the community center where I take painting classes. You can get what they call a G.E.D.—General Education Diploma, I think is what it means. Anyway, all you need to do is talk to a counselor and—"

"That's not it." Tate interrupted her harshly and ran a hand across his brow.

"Then what is it?" Abby asked, her smile determined.

Tate hesitated until the air between them was electric, like a storm ready to explode in the muggy heat.

"Where are you going with this discussion? What can I do to help? I don't understand." One minute Tate was exposing a painful part of his past, and the next he was growling at her. What was it with men? Something had been bothering him all evening. First he'd been restless and uneasy, then brooding and thoughtful, now angry. Nothing made sense.

And it wasn't going to. Abruptly he asked her if she was ready to leave.

He hardly said a word to her when he dropped her off at her apartment.

For a moment, Abby was convinced he'd never ask her out again.

"What about Sunday?" he finally said. "We can bring a picnic."

"Okay." But after this evening, Abby wasn't sure. He didn't sound as if he really wanted her company. "How about three o'clock?"

"Fine." His response was clipped.

Again he gave her a modest kiss, more a light brushing of their mouths than anything passionate or intense. Not a real kiss, in her opinion.

She leaned against the closed door of her apartment, not understanding why Tate was bothering to take her out. It seemed apparent that his interest in her wasn't romantic—although she didn't know what it actually was, didn't know what he wanted or needed from her. And for that matter, the bone-melting effect she'd experienced at their first meeting had long since gone. Tate was a handsome man, but he wasn't what she'd expected.

Maybe the grass wasn't so green after all.

After a restless Sunday morning, Abby decided that she'd go for a walk in the park. Logan often did before he came over to her place, and she hoped to run into him. She'd make a point of letting him know that their meeting was pure coincidence. They'd talk. Somehow she'd inform him, casually of course, that things weren't working out as she'd planned. In fact, yesterday, during her lesson with Mai-Ling, Tate hadn't come to the park, and she'd secretly been relieved. Despite today's picnic, she suspected that their romance was over before it could really start. And now she had doubts about its potential, anyway. Hmm. Maybe she'd hint to Logan that she missed his company. That should be enough to break the ice without either of them losing their pride. And that was what this came down to—pride.

The park was crowded by the time Abby arrived. Entering the grounds, she scanned the lawns for him and released a grateful sigh to find that he was sitting on a park bench reading. By himself. To her relief, Patty wasn't with him.

Deciding on her strategy, Abby stuck her hands in her pockets and strolled down the paved lane, hoping to look as if she'd merely come for a walk in the park. Their meeting would be by accident.

Abby stood about ten feet away, off to one side, watching Logan. She was surprised at the emotion she felt just studying him. He looked peaceful, but then he always did. He was composed, confident, in control. Equal to any situation. They'd been dating for almost a year and Abby hadn't realized that so much of her life was interwoven with Logan's. She'd taken him for granted until he was gone, and the emptiness he'd left behind had shocked her. She'd been stupid and insensitive. And heaven knew how difficult it was for her to admit she'd been wrong.

For several minutes Abby did nothing but watch him. A calm settled over her as she focused on Logan's shoulders. They weren't as broad or muscular as Tate's, but somehow it didn't matter. Not now, not when she was hurting, missing Logan and his friendship. Without giving it much thought, she'd been looking forward to Sunday all week and now she knew precisely why: Sundays had always been special because they were spent with Logan. It was Logan she wanted, Logan she needed, and Abby desperately hoped she wasn't too late.

Abby continued to gaze at him. After a while her determination to talk to him grew stronger. Never mind her pride— Logan had a right to know her feelings.

He'd been patient with her far longer than she deserved. Her stomach felt queasy, her mouth dry. Just when she gathered enough courage to approach him, Logan closed his book and stood up. Turning around he looked in her direction, but didn't hesitate for a second. He glanced at his watch and walked idly down the concrete pathway toward her until he was within calling distance. Abby's breath froze as he looked her way, blinked and looked in the opposite direction. She couldn't believe he'd purposely avoid her and she doubted he would've been able to see her standing off to the side.

The moment she was ready to step forward, Logan stopped to chat with two older men playing checkers. From her position, Abby saw them motion for him to sit down, which he did. He was soon deep in conversation with them. The three were obviously good friends, although she'd never met the other men before.

Abby loitered as long as she could. Half an hour passed and still Logan stayed.

Defeated, Abby realized she'd have to hurry or be late for her picnic with Tate. Silently she slipped from her viewing position and started across the grounds. When she glanced over her shoulder, she saw that Logan was alone on a bench again and watching a pair of young lovers kissing on the grass. Even from this distance, she saw a look of such intense pain cross his face, she had to force herself not to run to his side. He dropped his head in his hands and hunched forward as if a heavy burden was weighing on him.

Abby's throat clogged with tears until it was painful to breathe. They filled her eyes. Logan loved her and had loved her from the beginning, but she'd carelessly thrown his love aside. It had taken only a few days' separation to know with certainty that she loved him, too.

Tears rolled down her face, but Abby quickly brushed them aside. Logan wouldn't want to know she'd seen him. She'd stripped him of so much, it wouldn't be right to take his pride, as well. Today she'd tell Tate she wouldn't be seeing him again. If that was all Logan wanted, it would be a small price to pay. She'd run back to his arms and never leave him again.

By the time she got to her building, Tate was at the front door. They greeted each other and Tate told her about a special place he wanted to show her near Apple Valley.

She ran into her apartment to get a few things, then joined him in the car.

Both seemed preoccupied during the drive. Abby helped him unload the picnic basket, her thoughts racing at breakneck speed. She folded the tablecloth she'd brought over a picnic table while

Tate spread out a blanket under a shady tree. They hardly spoke.

"Abby—"

"Tate—"

They both began together.

"You first," Abby murmured and sat down, drawing up her legs and circling them with both arms, then resting her chin on her bent knees.

Tate remained standing, hands in his pockets as he paced. Again, something was obviously troubling him.

"Tate, what is it?"

"I didn't know it would be so hard to tell you," he said wryly and shook his head. "I meant to explain weeks ago."

What was he talking about?

His gaze settled on her, then flickered to the ground. "I tried to tell you Friday night after the movie, but I couldn't get the words out." He ran a weary hand over his face and fell to his knees at her side.

Abby reached for his hand and held it.

"Abby." He released a ragged breath. "*I can't read.* I'll pay you any amount if you'll teach me."

Five

In one brilliant flash everything about Tate fell into place. He hadn't been captivated by her charm and natural beauty. He'd overheard her teaching Mai-Ling how to read and knew she could help him. That was the reason he'd sought her out and cultivated a friendship. She could help him.

Small things became clear in her mind. No wonder Tate ordered the same thing she did in a restaurant. Naturally their date on Friday night had been awkward. He'd been trying to tell her then. How could she have been so blind?

Even now he studied her intently,

awaiting her response. His eyes glittered with pride, insecurity and fear. She recognized all those emotions and understood them now.

"Of course I'll teach you," she said reassuringly.

"I'll pay you anything you ask."

"Tate." Her grip on his hand tightened. "I wouldn't take anything. We're friends."

"But I can afford to pay you." He took a wad of bills from his pocket and breathed in slowly, glancing at the money in his hand.

Again Abby realized how difficult admitting his inability to read had been. "Put that away," Abby said calmly. "You won't be needing it."

Tate stuffed the bills back in his pocket. "You don't know how relieved I am to have finally told you," he muttered hoarsely.

"I don't think I could have been more obtuse," she said, still shocked at her own stupidity. "I'm amazed you've gotten along as well as you have. I was completely fooled."

"I've become adept at this. I've done it from the time I was in grade school."

"What happened?" Abby asked softly, although she could guess.

A sadness stole into his eyes. "I suppose it's because of all those times I was pulled out of school so we could move," he said unemotionally. "We left New Mexico in the middle of first grade and I never finished the year. Because I was tall for my age my mother put me in second grade the following September. The teacher wanted to hold me back but we moved again. And again and again." A bitterness infected his voice. "By the time I was in junior high and we'd moved to Minneapolis, I had devised all kinds of ways to disguise the fact that I couldn't read. I was the class clown, the troublemaker, the boy who'd do anything to get out of going to school."

"Oh, Tate." Her heart swelled with compassion.

Sitting beside her, Tate rubbed his hand across his face and smiled grimly. "But the hardest part was getting up the courage to tell you."

"You've never told anyone else, have you?"

"No. It was like admitting I have some horrible disease."

"You don't. We can fix this," she said. She was trying to reassure him and felt pathetically inadequate.

"Will you promise me that you'll keep this to yourself? For now?"

She nodded. "I promise." She understood how humiliated he felt, why he wanted his inability to read to remain a secret, and felt she had to agree.

"When can we start? There's so much I want to learn. So much I want to read. Books and magazines and computer programs..." He sounded eager, his gaze level and questioning.

"Is tomorrow too soon?" Abby asked. "I'd say it's about twenty years too late."

Tate brought Abby back to her apartment two hours later. Tomorrow she'd call the World Literacy Movement and have them email the forms for her to complete regarding Tate. He looked jubilant, excited. Telling her about his inability to read had probably been one of the most difficult things he'd ever done in his life. She understood how formidable his confession had felt to him because now she had to humble herself and call Logan. And that, although major to her, was a small thing in comparison.

Abby wasn't unhappy at Tate's confession. True, her pride was stung for a moment. But overall she was relieved. Tate was the kind of man who'd always attract women's attention. For a brief time she'd been caught up in his masculine appeal. And if it hadn't been for

Tate, it would have taken her a lot longer to recognize how fortunate she was to have Logan.

The thought of phoning him and admitting that she was wrong had been unthinkable a week ago. Had it only been a week? In some ways it felt like a year.

Abby glanced at the ceiling and prayed that Logan would answer her call. There was so much stored in her heart that she wanted to tell him. Her hand trembled as she lifted the receiver and tried to form positive thoughts. *Everything's going to work out. I know it will.* She repeated that mantra over and over as she dialed.

She was so nervous her fingers shook and her stomach churned until she was convinced she was going to be sick. Inhaling, Abby held her breath as his phone rang the first time. Her lungs refused to function. Abby closed her eyes tightly during the second ring.

"Hello."

Abby took a deep breath.

"Logan, this is Abby."

"Abby?" He sounded shocked.

"Can we talk? I mean, I can call back if this is inconvenient."

"I'm on my way out the door. Would you like me to come over?"

"Yes." She was surprised at how composed she sounded. "That would be great." She replaced the phone and tilted her head toward the ceiling. "Thank you," she murmured gratefully.

Looking down, Abby realized how casually she was dressed. When Logan saw her again, she wanted to bowl him over.

Racing into her room, she ripped the dress she'd worn Friday night off the hanger, then decided it wouldn't do. She tossed it across her bed. She tried on one outfit and then another. Never had she been more unsure about what she wanted to wear. Finally she chose a pair of tailored black pants and a white blouse with an eyelet collar. Simple, elegant, classic.

Abby was frantically brushing her hair when the buzzer went. *Logan.* She gripped the edge of the sink and took in a deep breath. Then she set down the brush, practiced her smile and walked into the living room.

"Hello, Abby," Logan said a moment later as he stepped into the apartment.

Her first impulse was to throw her arms around him and weep. A tightness gripped her throat. Whatever poise she'd managed to gather was shaken and gone with one look from him.

"Hello, Logan. Would you like to sit down?" She gestured toward the chair. Her gaze was fixed on his shoulders as he walked across the room and took a seat.

"And before you ask," he interjected sternly, "no, I don't want anything to drink. Sit down, Abby."

She complied, grateful because she didn't know how much longer her knees would support her.

"You wanted to talk?" The lines at the side of his mouth deepened, but he wasn't smiling.

"Yes." She laced her hands together tightly. "I was wrong," she murmured. Now that the words were out, Abby experienced none of the calm she'd expected. "I'm—I'm sorry."

"It wasn't a question of my being right or your being wrong," Logan said. "I'm not looking for an apology."

Abby's lips trembled and she bit into the bottom corner. "I know that. But I felt I owed you one."

"No." He stood and with one hand in his pocket paced the width of the carpet. "That's not what I wanted to hear. I told you to call me when you were sure it was me you wanted and not Tate." His eyes rested on her, his expression hooded.

Abby stood, unable to meet his gaze. "I *am* sure," she breathed. "I know it's you I want."

His mouth quirked in what could have

been a smile, but he didn't acknowledge her confession.

"You have every right to be angry with me." She couldn't look at him, afraid of what she'd see. If he were to reject her now, Abby didn't think she could stand it. "I've missed you so much," she mumbled. Her cheeks flamed with color, and she couldn't believe how difficult this was. She felt tears in her eyes as she bowed her head.

"Abby." Logan's arms came around her shoulders, bringing her within the comforting circle of his arms. He lifted her chin and lovingly studied her face. "You're sure?"

The growing lump in her throat made speech impossible. She nodded, letting all the love in her eyes say the words.

"Oh, Abby…" He claimed her lips with a hungry kiss that revealed the depth of his feelings.

Slipping her arms around his neck, Abby felt him shudder with a longing he'd suppressed all these months. He buried his face in the dark waves of her hair and held her so tightly it was difficult to breathe.

"I've been so wrong about so many things," she confessed, rubbing her hands up and down his spine, reveling in the muscular feel of him.

Lowering himself to the sofa, Logan pulled Abby onto his lap. His warm breath was like a gentle caress as she wound her arms around his neck and kissed him, wanting to make up to him for all the pain she'd caused them both. The wild tempo of her pulse made clear thought impossible.

Finally, Logan dragged his mouth from hers. "You're sure?" he asked as if he couldn't quite believe it.

Abby pressed her forehead against his shoulder and nodded. "Very sure. I was such a fool."

His arm held her securely in place. "Tell me more. I'm enjoying this."

Unable to resist, Abby kissed the side of his mouth. "I thought you would."

"So you missed me?"

"I was miserable."

"Good!"

"Logan," she cried softly. "It wouldn't do you any harm to tell me how lonely *you* were."

"I wasn't," he said jokingly.

Involuntarily Abby stiffened and swallowed back the hurt. "I know. Patty mentioned that you'd taken her to the Twins game."

Logan smiled wryly. "We went with several other people."

"It bothers me that you could see someone else so soon."

"Honey." His hold tightened around her waist, bringing her closer. "It wasn't like you're thinking."

"But…you said you weren't lonely."

"How could I have been? I saw you Tuesday and then at the game on Wednesday."

"I know, but—"

"Are we going to argue?"

"A thousand kisses might convince me," she teased and rested her head on his shoulder.

"I haven't got the willpower to continue kissing you without thinking of other things," he murmured in her ear as his hand stroked her hair. "I love you, Abby. I've loved you from the first time I asked you out." His breathing seemed less controlled than it had been a moment before.

"Oh, Logan." Fresh tears sprang to her eyes. She started to tell him how much she cared for him, but he went on, cutting off her words.

"As soon as I saw Tate I knew there was no way I could compete with him. He's everything I'll never be. Tall. Movie-star looks." He shook his head. "I don't blame you for being attracted to him."

Abby straightened so she could look

at this man she loved. Her hands framed his face. "You're a million things Tate could never be."

"I know this has been hard on you."

"But I was so stupid," Abby inserted.

He kissed her lightly, his lips lingering over hers. "I can't help feeling grateful that you won't be seeing him again."

Abby lowered her eyes. She *would* be seeing Tate, but not in the way Logan meant.

A stillness filled the room. "Abby?"

She gave him a feeble smile.

"You aren't seeing Tate, are you?"

She couldn't reveal Tate's problem to anyone. She'd promised. And not for the world would she embarrass him, especially when admitting he couldn't read had been so difficult. No matter how much she wanted to tell Logan, she couldn't.

"I'd like to explain," Abby replied, her voice trembling.

Logan stiffened and lightly pushed her

from his lap. "I don't want explanations. All I want is the truth. Will you or will you not be seeing Tate?"

"Not romantically," she answered, as tactfully and truthfully as possible.

Logan's eyes hardened. "What other explanation could there be?"

"I can't tell you that," she said forcefully and stood up.

"Of course you can." A muscle worked in his jaw. "We're right back where we started, aren't we, Abby?"

"No." She felt like screaming at him for being so unreasonable. Surely he recognized how hard it had been for her to call him and admit she was wrong?

"Will you stop seeing Tate, then?" he challenged.

"I can't." Her voice cracked in a desperate appeal for him to understand. "We live in the same neighborhood..." she said, stalling for time as her mind raced for an excuse. "I'll probably run into him.... I mean, it'd be only natural, since he's so close and all."

"Abby," Logan groaned impatiently. "That's not what I mean and you know it. Will you or will you not be *seeing* Tate?"

She hesitated. Knowing what her promise was doing to her relationship with Logan, Tate would want him to know. But she couldn't say anything without clearing it with him first.

"Abby?"

"I'll be seeing him, but please understand that it's not the way you assume."

For an instant, Abby saw pain in Logan's eyes. The pain she witnessed was the same torment she was experiencing herself.

They stood with only a few feet separating them and yet Abby felt they'd never been further apart. Whole worlds seemed to loom between them. Logan's ego was at stake, his pride, and he didn't want her to continue seeing Tate, no matter what the reason.

"You won't stop seeing him," Logan challenged furiously.

"I can't," Abby cried, just as angry.

"Then there's nothing left to say."

"Yes," Abby said, "there is, but you're in no mood to hear it. Just remember that things aren't always as they appear."

"Goodbye, Abby," he responded. "And next time don't bother calling me unless—"

Abby stalked across the room and threw open the door. "Next time I won't," she said with a cutting edge.

Reaction set in the minute the door slammed behind him. Abby was so angry that pacing the floor did little to relieve it. How could Logan say he loved her in one breath and turn around and storm out the next? Yet, he'd done exactly that.

Once the anger dissipated, Abby began to tremble and felt the tears burning for

release. Pride demanded that she fore-
stall them. She wouldn't allow Logan
to reduce her to that level. She shook
her head and kept her chin raised. She
wouldn't cry, she wouldn't cry, she repeated over and over as one tear after
another slid down her cheeks.

"Who did you say was responsible
for the literacy movement?" Tate asked,
leafing respectfully through the first
book.

"Dr. Frank Laubach. He was a mis-
sionary in the Philippines in the 1920s.
At that time some of the island people
didn't have a written language. He in-
vented one and later developed a method
of teaching adults to read."

"Sounds like he accomplished a lot."

Abby nodded. "By the time he died in
1970, his work had spread to 105 coun-
tries and 313 languages."

Tate continued leafing through the
pages of the primary workbook. Abby

wanted to start him at the most funda-
mental skill level, knowing his progress
would be rapid. At this point, Tate would
need all the encouragement he could get
and the speed with which he completed
the lower-level books was sure to help.

Abby hadn't underestimated Tate's enthusiasm. By the end of the first lesson
he had relearned the alphabet and was
reading simple phrases. Proudly he took
the book home with him.

"Can we meet again tomorrow?" he
asked, standing near her apartment door.

"I've got my class tomorrow evening,"
Abby explained, "but if you like, we
could meet for a half hour before—or
after if you prefer."

"Before, I think."

The following afternoon, Tate showed
up an hour early, just after she got home
from work, and seemed disappointed
that Abby would be occupied with softball on Wednesday evening.

"We could get together afterward if you want," she told him.

Affectionately, Tate kissed her on the cheek. "I want."

Again she noted that his fondness for her was more like that of a brother—or a pupil for his teacher. She was grateful for that, at least. And he was wonderful to her. He brought over takeout meals and gave her small gifts as a way of showing his appreciation. The gifts weren't necessary, but they salvaged Tate's pride and that was something she was learning more about every day—male pride.

Abby was dressing for the game Wednesday evening when the phone rang. No longer did she expect or even hope it would be Logan. He'd made his position completely clear. Fortunately, call display told her it was her parents' number.

"Hello, Mom."

"Abby, I've been worried about you."

"I'm fine!" She forced some enthusiasm into her voice.

"Oh, dear, it's worse than I thought."

"What's worse?"

"Logan and you."

"There is no more Logan and me," she returned.

A strained silence followed. "But I thought—"

"Listen, Mom," Abby cut in, unwilling to listen to her mother's postmortem. "I've got a game tonight. Can I call you later?"

"Why don't you come over for dinner?"

"Not tonight." Abby hated to turn down her mother's invitation, but she'd already agreed to see Tate for his next lesson.

"It's your birthday Friday," Glenna reminded her.

"I'll come for dinner then," Abby said with a feeble smile. Her birthday was only two days away and she wasn't in any mood to celebrate. "But only if you promise to make my favorite dish."

"Barbecued chicken!" her mother announced. "You bet."

"And, Mom," Abby continued, "you were right about Logan."

"What was I right about?" Her mother's voice rose slightly.

"He does love me, and I love him."

Abby thought she heard a small, happy sound.

"What made you realize that?" her mother asked.

"A lot of things," Abby said noncommittally. "But I also realized that loving someone doesn't make everything perfect. I wish it did."

"I have the feeling there's something important you're not telling me, Abby," Glenna said on a note of puzzled sadness. "But I know you will in your own good time."

Abby couldn't disagree with her mother's observation. "I'll be at your place

around six on Friday," she murmured.
"And thanks, Mom."

"What are mothers for?" Glenna
teased.

The disconnected phone line droned
in Abby's ear before she hung up, suddenly surprised to see that it was time
to head over to the park. For the first
time that she could remember, she didn't
feel psyched up for the game. She wasn't
ready to see Logan, which would be
more painful than reassuring. And if he
paid Patty special attention, Abby didn't
know how she'd handle that. But Logan
wouldn't do anything to hurt her. At least
she knew him well enough to be sure
of that.

The first thing Abby noticed as she
walked onto the diamond was that Patty
Martin had cut and styled her hair. The
transformation from straight mousy-
brown hair to short, bouncy curls was

astonishing. The young woman posi-
tively glowed.

"What do you think?" Patty asked in
a hurried voice. "Your hair is always so
pretty and…" She let the rest of what she
was going to say fade.

Abby held herself motionless. Patty
had made herself attractive for Logan.
She desperately wanted Logan's interest,
and for all Abby knew, she was getting
it. "I think you look great," Abby commented, unable to deny the truth or to
be unkind.

"I was scared out of my wits," Patty
admitted shyly. "It's been a long time
since I was at the hairdresser's."

"Hey, Patty, they're waiting for you
on the field," the team's coach hollered.
"Abby, you, too."

"Okay, Dick," Patty called back happily, her eyes shining. "I've gotta go.
We'll talk later, okay?"

"Fine." Softening her stiff mitt against

her hand with unnecessary force, Abby ran to her position at first base.

Logan was practicing in the outfield.

"Abby," he called, and when she turned, she found his gaze level and unwavering. "Catch."

Nothing appeared to affect him. They'd suffered through the worst four days of their relationship and he looked at her as coolly and unemotionally as he would a…a dish of potato salad. She didn't respond other than to catch the softball and pitch it to second base.

The warm-up period lasted for about ten minutes. Abby couldn't recall a time she'd felt less like playing, and it showed.

"What's the matter, Ab?" Dick asked her at the bottom of the fifth after she'd struck out for the third time. "You're not yourself tonight."

"I'm sorry," she said with a frustrated sigh. Her eyes didn't meet his. "This isn't one of my better nights."

"She's got other things on her mind."

Logan spoke from behind her, signaling that he was sitting in the bleachers one row above. "Her boyfriend just showed up, so she'll do better."

Abby whirled around to face Logan. "What do you mean by that?"

Logan nodded in the direction of the parking lot. Abby's gaze followed his movement and she wanted to groan aloud. Tate was walking toward the stands.

"Tate isn't my boyfriend," Abby's voice was taut with impatience.

"Oh, is that terminology passé?" Logan returned.

Stunned at the bitterness in him, Abby found no words to respond. They were both hurting, and in their pain they were lashing out at each other.

Logan slid from the bleachers for his turn at bat. Abby focused her attention on him, deciding she didn't want to make a fuss over Tate's unexpected arrival.

Logan swung wildly at the first pitch,

hitting the ball with the tip of his bat. Abby could hear the wood crack as the ball went flying over the fence for a home run. Logan looked as shocked as Abby. He tossed the bat aside and ran around the bases to the shouts and cheers of his teammates. Abby couldn't remember Logan ever getting more than a single.

"Hi." Tate slid into the row of seats behind her. "You don't mind if I come and watch, do you?" he asked as he leaned forward with lazy grace.

"Not at all," Abby said blandly. It didn't make any difference now. She stared at her laced fingers, attempting to fight off the depression that seemed to have settled over her. She was so caught up in her own sorrows that she didn't see the accident. Only the startled cries of those around her alerted her to the fact that something had happened.

"What's wrong?" Abby asked frantically as the bench cleared. Everyone was running toward Patty, who was clutching her arm and doubled over in pain.

Logan's voice could be heard above the confusion. "Stand back. Give her room." Gently he aided Patty into a sitting position.

Even to Abby's untrained eye it was obvious that Patty's arm was broken. Logan tore off his shirt and tied it around her upper body to create a sling and support the injured arm.

The words *hospital* and *doctor* were flying around, but everyone seemed stunned and no one moved. Again it was Logan who helped Patty to her feet and led her to his car. His calm, decisive actions imparted confidence to both teams. Only minutes before, Abby had been angry because he displayed so little emotion.

"What happened?" Abby asked Dick as they walked off the field.

"I'm not sure." Dick looked shaken himself. "Patty was trying to steal a base and collided with the second baseman. When she fell, she put out her arm to catch herself and it twisted under her."

"Will she be all right?"

"Logan seemed to think so. He's taking her to the emergency room. He said he'd let us know her condition as soon as possible."

The captain of the opposing team crossed the diamond to talk to Dick and it was decided that they'd play out the remainder of the game.

But without Logan the team was short one male player.

"Do you think your friend would mind filling in?" Dick asked somewhat sheepishly, glancing at Tate.

"I can ask."

"No problem," Tate said, smiling as he picked up Logan's discarded mitt and ran onto the field.

Although they'd decided to finish the game, almost everyone was preoccupied with the accident. Abby's team ended up winning, thanks to Tate, but only by a slight margin.

The group as a whole proceeded to the pizza parlor to wait for word about Patty.

Tate sat across the long wooden table from Abby, chatting easily with her fellow teammates. Only a few slices of the two large pizzas had been eaten. Their conversation was a low hum as they recounted their versions of the accident and what could have been done to prevent it.

Abby was grateful for Logan's clear thinking and quick actions. He wasn't the kind of skilled softball player who'd stand out, but he gave of himself in a way that was essential to every member of the team. Only a few days earlier she'd found Logan lacking. Compared to the muscular Tate, he'd seemed a poor second. Now she noted that his strengths were inner ones. Again she was reminded that if given the chance, she would love this man for the rest of her life.

Abby didn't see Logan enter the restaurant, but the immediate clamor caused her to turn. She stood with the others.

"Patty's fine," he assured everyone. "Her arm's broken, but I don't think that's news to anyone."

"When will she be back?"

"We want to send flowers or something."

"When do you think she'll feel up to company?"

Everyone spoke at once. Calmly Logan answered each question and when he'd finished, the mood around the table was considerably lighter.

A tingling awareness at the back of her neck told Abby that Logan was near. With a sweeping action he swung his foot over the long bench and joined her.

He focused on Tate, sitting across from Abby. "I wish I could say it's good

to see you again," he said with stark un-
friendliness.

"Logan, please!" Abby hissed.

The two men eyed each other like
bears who'd violated each other's terri-
tory. Tate had no romantic interest in her,
Abby was convinced of that, but Logan
was openly challenging him and Tate
wouldn't walk away from such blatant
provocation.

Unaware of the dangerous undercur-
rents swirling around the table, Dick
Snyder sauntered over and slapped
Logan on the back.

"We owe a debt of thanks to Tate
here," he informed Logan cheerfully.
"He stepped in for you when you were
gone. He batted in the winning run."

Logan and Tate didn't so much as
blink. "Tate's been doing a lot of that
for me lately, isn't that right, Abby?"

Wrenching her gaze from him, Abby
stood and, with as much dignity and

pride as she could muster, walked out of the restaurant and went home alone.

The phone was ringing when she walked into the apartment. Abby let it ring. She didn't want to talk to anyone. She didn't even want to know who'd called.

"Abby, would you take the bread out of the oven?" her mother asked, walking out to the patio.

"Okay." Abby turned off the broiler and pulled out the cookie sheet, on which slices of French bread oozed with melted butter and chopped garlic. Her enthusiasm for this birthday celebration was nil.

The doorbell caught her by surprise. "Are you expecting anyone?" she asked her mother, who'd returned to the kitchen.

"Not that I know of. I'll get it."

Abby was placing the bread slices in

a warming basket when she heard her mother's surprised voice.

Turning, Abby looked straight at Logan.

Six

A shocked expression crossed Logan's face. "Abby." He took a step inside the room and paused.

"Hello, Logan." A tense silence ensued as Abby primly folded her hands.

"I'll check the chicken," Glenna Carpenter murmured discreetly as she hurried past them.

"What brings you to this neck of the woods?" Abby forced a lightness into her voice. He looked tired, as if he hadn't been sleeping well. For that matter, neither had Abby, but she doubted either would admit as much.

Logan handed her a wrapped package.

"I wanted your mother to give you this. But since you're here—happy birthday."

A small smile parted her trembling lips as Abby accepted the brightly wrapped gift. He had come to her parents' home to deliver this, but he hadn't expected her to be there.

"Thank you." She continued to hold it.

"I, uh, didn't expect to see you." He stated the obvious, as though he couldn't think of anything else to say.

"Where else would I be on my birthday?"

Logan shrugged. "With Tate."

Abby released a sigh of indignation. "I thought I'd explained that I'm not involved with Tate. We're friends, nothing more."

She shook her head. They'd gone over this before. Another argument wouldn't help. Abby figured she'd endured enough emotional turmoil in the past few weeks. She still hadn't spoken to Tate about telling Logan the truth. But she couldn't, not with Tate feeling as sensitive as he did about the whole thing.

"Abby." Logan's voice was deadly quiet. "Don't you see what's happening? You may not think of Tate in a romantic light, but I saw the way he was looking at you in the pizza place."

"You openly challenged him." Abby threw out a few challenges of her own. "How did you expect him to react? You wouldn't have behaved any differently," she said. "And if you've come to ruin my birthday…then you can just leave. I've had about all I can take from you, Logan Fletcher." She whirled around, not wanting to face him.

"I didn't come for that." The defeat was back in his voice again.

Abby's pulse thundered in her ears as she waited for the sounds of him leaving—at the same time hoping he wouldn't.

"Aren't you going to open your present?" he said at last.

Abby turned and wiped away a tear that had escaped from the corner of her eye. "I already know what it is," she said, glancing down at the package. "Honestly, Logan, you're so predictable."

"How could you possibly know?"

"Because you got me the same perfume for my birthday last year." Deftly she removed the wrapping paper and held up the small bottle of expensive French fragrance.

"I like the way it smells on you," Logan murmured, walking across the room. He rested his hands on her shoulders. "And if I'm so predictable, you'll also recall that there's a certain thank-you I expect."

Any resistance drained from her as Logan pulled her into his embrace. Abby slid her arms around his neck and tasted the sweetness of his kiss. A wonderful languor stole through her limbs as his mouth brushed the sweeping curve of her lashes and burned a trail down her cheek to her ear.

"I love you, Logan," Abby whispered with all the intensity in her.

Logan went utterly still. Gradually he raised his head so he could study her. Unflinching, Abby met his gaze determined that he see for himself what her eyes and heart were saying.

"If you love me, then you'll stop seeing Tate," he said flatly.

"And if you love *me,* you'll trust me."

"Abby." Logan dropped his hands and stepped away. "I—"

"Oh, Logan." Glenna Carpenter moved out of the kitchen. "I'm glad to see you're still here. We insist you stay for dinner. Isn't that right, Abby?"

Logan held her gaze with mesmerizing simplicity.

"Of course we do. If you don't have another appointment," Abby said meaningfully.

"You know I don't."

Abby knew nothing of the kind, but didn't want to argue. "Did you see the gift Logan brought me?" Abby asked her mother and held out the perfume.

"Logan is always so thoughtful."

"Yes, he is," Abby agreed and slipped an arm around his waist, enjoying the feel of him at her side. "Thoughtful, but not very original." Her eyes smiled into his, pleading with him that, for tonight, they could forget their differences.

Logan's arms slid just as easily around her. "But with that kind of thank-you, what incentive do I have for shopping around?"

Abby laughed and led the way to the back patio.

Frank Carpenter, Abby's father, was busy standing in front of the barbecue, basting chicken.

"Logan," he exclaimed and held out a welcoming hand. "This is a pleasant surprise. Good to see you."

Logan and her father had always gotten along and had several interests in common. For a time that had irked Abby. Defiantly she'd wanted to make it clear that she wouldn't marry a man solely because her parents thought highly of him. Her childish attitude had changed dramatically these past weeks.

Abby's mother brought another place setting from the kitchen to add to the three already on the picnic table. Abby made several more trips into the kitchen to carry out the salad, toasted bread and a glass of wine for Logan.

Absently, Logan accepted the glass from her and smiled, deep in conversation with her father. Happiness washed over Abby as she munched on a potato chip. Looking at the two of them now—Abby busy helping her mother and Logan chatting easily with her father—she figured there was little to distinguish them as unmarried.

Dinner and the time that followed were cheerful. Frank suggested a game of cards while they were eating birthday cake and ice cream. But Abby's mother immediately rejected the idea.

"I think Glenna's trying to tell me to keep my mouth shut because it's obvious you two want some time alone," Abby's father complained.

"I'm saying no such thing," Glenna denied instantly as an embarrassed flush brightened her cheeks. "We were young once, Frank."

"Once!" Frank scolded. "I don't know about you, but I'm not exactly ready for the grave."

"We'll play cards another time," Logan promised, ending a friendly argument between her parents.

"Double-deck pinochle," Frank prompted. "Best card game there is."

Glenna pretended to agree but rolled her eyes dramatically when Frank wasn't looking.

"Shall we?" Logan successfully contained a smile and held out his open palm to Abby. She placed her hand in his, more contented than she could ever remember being. After their farewells to her parents, Logan followed her back to her apartment, parking his car beside hers. He took a seat while Abby hurried into the next room.

"Give me a minute to freshen up," Abby called out as she ran a brush through her hair and studied her reflection in the bathroom mirror. She looked happy. The sparkle was back in her eyes.

She dabbed some of the perfume Logan had given her to the pulse points at her throat and wrists. Maybe this would garner even more of a reaction. He wasn't one to display a lot of emotion, but he seemed to be coming along nicely in that area. His kisses had produced an overwhelming physical response in Abby, and she was aware that his feeling for her ran deep and strong. It had been only a matter of weeks ago that she'd wondered why he bothered to kiss her at all.

"I suppose you're going to suggest we drive to Des Moines and back," Logan teased when she joined him a few minutes later.

"Logan!" she cried, feigning excitement. "That's a wonderful idea."

He rolled his eyes and and laid the paper on the sofa. "How about a movie instead?"

Abby gave a fake groan. "So predictable."

"I've been wanting to see this one." He pointed at an ad for the movie she'd seen with Tate.

"I've already been," Abby tossed back, not thinking.

"When?"

Abby could feel the hostility exuding from Logan. He knew. Without a word he'd guessed that Abby had been to the movie with Tate.

"Not long ago." She tried desperately

to put the evening back on an even keel. "But I'd see it again. The film's great."

The air between them became heavy and oppressive.

"Forget the movies," Logan said and neatly folded the paper. He straightened and stalked to the far side of the room. "In fact, why don't we forget everything."

Hands clenched angrily at her side, Abby squared her shoulders. "If you ruin my birthday, Logan Fletcher, I don't think I'll ever forgive you."

His expression was cold and unreadable. "Yes, but there's always Tate."

A hysterical sob rose in her throat, but Abby managed to choke it off. "I...I told you tonight that I loved you." Her voice wobbled treacherously as her eyes pleaded with his. "Doesn't that mean anything to you? Anything at all?"

Logan's gaze raked her from head to foot. "Only that you don't know the meaning of the word. You want both

Tate *and* me, Abby. But you can't decide between us so you'd prefer to keep us both dangling until you make up your mind." His voice gained volume with each word. "But I won't play that game."

Abby breathed in sharply as a fiery anger burned in her cheeks. Once she would have ranted, cried and hurled her own accusations. Now she stood stunned and disbelieving. "If you honestly believe that, then there's nothing left to say." Her voice was calmer than she dared hope. Life seemed filled with ironies all of a sudden. Outwardly she presented a clearheaded composure while on the inside she felt a fiery pain. Perhaps for the first time in her life she was acting completely selflessly, and this was her reward—losing Logan.

Without another word, Logan walked across the room and out the front door.

Abby watched him leave with a sense of unreality. This couldn't be happening to her. Not on her birthday. Last year

Logan had taken her to dinner at L'Hôtel Sofitel and given her—what else—perfume. A hysterical bubble of laughter slipped from her. He was predictable, but so loving and caring. She remembered how they'd danced until midnight and gone for a stroll in the moonlight. Only a year ago, Logan had made her birthday the most perfect day of her life. But this year he was ruining it.

Angry, hurt and agitated, Abby paced the living-room carpet until she thought she'd go mad. Dano had wandered into the living room when she and Logan came in, but had disappeared into her bedroom once he sensed tension. Figured. Not even her cat was interested in comforting her. Usually when she was upset she'd ride her bike or do something physical. But bike riding at night could be dangerous, so she'd go running instead. She changed into old jeans and a faded sweatshirt that had a picture of a Disneyland castle on the front. She had trouble locating her second tennis shoe, then threw it aside in disgust when the rainbow-colored lace snapped in two.

She sighed. Nothing had gone right today. Tate had been disappointed that she wasn't able to meet him. Because of that, she'd been fighting off a case of guilt when she went to her parents'. Then Logan had shown up, and everything had steadily and rapidly gone downhill.

Ripping a lace from one of her baseball shoes, Abby had to wrap it around the sole of the shoe several times. On her way out the door, she paused and returned to the bathroom. If she was going to go running, then she'd do it smelling better than any other runner in Minneapolis history. She'd dabbed perfume on every exposed part of her body when she stepped out the door.

A light drizzle had begun to fall. Terrific. A fitting end to a rotten day.

The first block was a killer. She couldn't be that badly out of shape, could she? She rode her bike a lot. And wasn't her running speed the best on the team?

The second block, Abby forced her mind off how out of breath she was becoming. Logan's buying her perfume made her chuckle. *Predictable. Reliable. Confident.* They were all words that adequately described Logan. But so were *unreasonable* and *stubborn*—traits she'd only seen recently.

The drizzle was followed by a cloudburst and Abby's hair and clothes were plastered against her in the swirling wind and rain. She shouldn't be laughing. But she did anyway as she raced back to her apartment. It was either laugh or cry, and laughing seemed to come naturally. Laughing made her feel better than succumbing to tears.

By the time Abby returned to her building, she was drenched and shivering. With her chin tucked under and her arms folded around her middle, she fought off the chill and hurried across the parking lot. She was almost at her building door when she realized she didn't have the keys. She'd locked herself out!

What more could go wrong? she wondered. Maybe the superintendent was home. She stepped out in the rain to see if the lights were on in his apartment, which was situated above hers. His place was dark. Of course. That was how everything else was going.

Cupping one hand over her mouth while the other held her stomach, Abby's laughter was mixed with sobs of anger and frustration.

"Abby?" Logan's urgent voice came from the street. Hurriedly he crossed it, took one look at her and hauled her into his arms.

"Logan, I'll get you wet," she cried, trying to push herself free.

"What happened? Are you all right?"

"No. Yes. I don't know," she murmured, sniffling miserably. "What are you doing here?"

Logan brought her out of the rain and stood with his back blocking the wind, trying to protect her from the storm. "Let's get you inside and dry and I'll explain."

"Why?" she asked and wrung the water from the hem of her sweatshirt. "So you can hurl insults at me?"

"No," he said vehemently. "I've been half-crazy wondering where you were."

"I'll just bet," Abby taunted unmercifully. "I'm surprised you didn't assume I was with Tate."

A grimace tightened his jaw, and Abby knew she'd hit her mark. "Are you going to be difficult or are we going inside to talk this out reasonably?"

"We can't go inside," she said.

"Why not?"

"Because I forgot my keys."

"Oh, Abby," Logan groaned.

"And the manager's gone. Do you have any more bright ideas?"

"Did you leave the bedroom window open?" he asked with marked patience.

"Yes, just a little, but—" A glimmer of an idea sparked and she smiled boldly at Logan. "Follow me."

"Why do I have the feeling I'm not going to like this?" he asked under his breath as Abby pulled him by the hand around to the back of the building.

"Here," she said, bending her knee and lacing her fingers together to give him a boost upward to the slightly open window.

"You don't expect to launch me through there, do you?" Logan glared at her. "I won't fit."

Rivulets of rain trickled down the back of Abby's neck. "Well, I can't do it. You know I'm afraid of heights."

"Abby, the window's barely five feet off the ground."

"I'm standing here, drenched and

miserable," she said, waving her hands wildly. "On my birthday, no less," she added sarcastically, "and you don't want to rescue me."

"I'm not in the hero business," Logan muttered as he hunched his shoulders to ward off the rain. "Try Tate."

"Fine, I'll do that." She stalked off to the side of the building.

"Abby?" He sounded unsure as she dragged over an aluminum garbage can.

"Go away!" she shouted. "I don't need you."

"What's the difference between going through the window using a garbage can or having me lift you through?"

"Plenty." She wasn't sure what, but she didn't want to take the time to figure it out. All she wanted was a hot bath and ten gallons of hot chocolate.

"You're being totally irrational."

"I've always been irrational. It's never bothered you before." Her voice trembled as she balanced her weight on the lid of the garbage can. She reached the window and pushed it open enough to crawl through when she felt the garbage can lid give way. "Logan!" she screamed, terror gripping her as she started to fall.

Instantly he was there. His arms gripped her waist as she tumbled off the aluminum container. Together they went crashing to the ground, Logan twisting so he took the worst of the fall.

"Are you okay?" he asked frantically, straightening and brushing the hair from her face.

Abby was too stunned and breathless to speak, so she just nodded.

"Now listen," he whispered angrily. "I'm going to lift you up to the windowsill and that's final. Do you understand?"

She nodded again.

"I've had enough of this arguing. I'm cold and wet and I want to get inside and talk some reason into you." He stood and wiped the mud from his hands, then helped her up. Taking the position she had earlier, he crouched and let her use his knee as a step as his laced fingers boosted her to the level of the window.

Abby fell into the bedroom with a loud thud, knocking the lamp off her nightstand. Dano howled in terror and dashed under the bed.

"Are you okay?" Logan yelled from outside.

Abby stuck her head out the window. "Fine. Come around to the front and I'll let you in."

"I'll meet you at your door."

"Logan." She leaned forward and smiled at him provocatively. "You *are* my hero."

He didn't look convinced. "Sure. Whatever you say."

Abby had buzzed open the front door and unlocked her own by the time he came around the building. His wet hair was dripping water down his face, and his shirt was plastered to his chest, revealing a lean, muscular strength. He looked as drenched and miserable as she felt.

"You take a shower while I drive home and change out of these." He looked down ruefully at his mud-spattered beige pants and rain-soaked shirt.

Abby agreed. Logan had turned and was halfway out the door when Abby called him back. "Why are you here?" she asked, wanting to delay his leaving.

He shrugged and gave her that warm, lazy smile she loved. "I don't know. I thought there might be another movie you wanted to see."

Abby laughed and blew him a kiss. "I'm sure there is."

When Logan returned forty minutes later, Abby's hair was washed and blown dry and hung in a long French braid down the middle of her back. She'd changed into a multicolored bulky sweater and jeans.

Abby smiled. "We're not going to fight, are we?"

"I certainly hope not!" he exclaimed. "I don't think I can take much more of this. When I left here the first time I was thinking..." He paused and scratched his head. "I was actually entertaining the thought of driving to Des Moines and back."

"That's crazy." Abby tried unsuccessfully to hide her giggles.

"You're telling me?" He sat on the sofa and held out his arm to her, silently inviting her to join him.

Abby settled on the sofa, her head resting on his chest while his hand caressed her shoulder.

"Do you recall how uncomplicated our lives were just a few weeks ago?" Logan asked her.

"Dull. Ordinary."

"What changed all that?"

Abby was hesitant to bring Tate's name into the conversation. "Life, I guess," she answered vaguely. "I know you may misunderstand this," she added in a husky murmur, "but I don't want to go back to the way our relationship was then." He hadn't told her he loved her and she hadn't recognized the depth of her own feelings.

He didn't move. "No, I don't suppose you would."

Abby repositioned her head and placed the palm of her hand on his jaw, turning his face so she could study him. Their eyes met. The hard, uncompromising look in his dark eyes disturbed her. She desperately wanted to assure him of her love. But she'd realized after the first time that words were inadequate. She shifted and slid her hands over his chest to pause at his shoulders.

The brilliance of his eyes searched her face. "Abby." He groaned her name as he fiercely claimed her lips. His hand found its way to the nape of her neck, his fingers gently pulling dark strands free from the braid so he could twine them through his fingers.

His breathing deep, he buried his face in the slope of her neck. "Just let me hold you for a while. Let's not talk."

She agreed and settled into the warm comfort of his embrace. The staccato beat of his heart gradually returned to a normal pace and Abby felt content and loved. The key to a peaceful relationship was to bask in their love for each other, she thought, smiling. That, and not saying a word.

"What's so amusing?" Logan asked, his breath stirring the hair at the side of her face.

"How do you know I'm smiling?"

"I can feel it."

Abby tilted her head so she could look into his eyes. "This turned into a happy birthday, after all," she said.

Now he smiled, too. "Can I see you tomorrow?"

"If you weren't going to ask me, then I would've been forced to make some wild excuse to see *you*." Lovingly Abby rubbed her hand along the side of his jaw, enjoying the slightly prickly feel of his beard.

"What would you like to do?"

"I don't care as long as I'm with you."

"My, my," he whispered, taking her hand. Tenderly he kissed her palm. "You're much easier to please than I remember."

"You don't know the half of it," she teased.

Logan stiffened and sat upright. "What's tomorrow?"

"The tenth. Why?"

"I can't, Abby. I've got something scheduled."

She felt a rush of disappointment but knew that if she was frustrated, so was Logan. "Don't worry, I'll survive," she assured him, then smiled. "At least I think I will."

"But don't plan anything for the day after tomorrow."

"Of course I'm planning something."

"Abby." He sounded tired and impatient.

"Well, it's Sunday, right? Our usual day. So I'm planning to spend it with you. I thought that was what you wanted."

"I do."

The grimness about his mouth relaxed.

Almost immediately afterward, Logan appeared restless and uneasy. Later, as she dressed for bed, she convinced herself that it was her imagination.

The lesson with Mai-Ling the following afternoon went well. It was the last reading session they'd have, since Mai-Ling was now ready to move on. She'd scheduled one with Tate right afterward, deciding that what Logan didn't know wouldn't hurt him. Tate was still painfully self-conscious and uncomfortable about telling anyone else, although his progress was remarkable and he advanced more quickly than any student she'd ever tutored, including the talented

Mai-Ling. From experience, she could tell he was spending many hours each evening studying.

On her way back to her apartment late Saturday afternoon, Abby decided on the spur of the moment to stop at Patty's and see how she was recuperating. She'd sent her an email wishing her a rapid recovery and had promised to stop over some afternoon. Patty needed friends and Abby was feeling generous. Her topsy-turvy world had been righted.

She went to a drugstore first and bought half a dozen glossy magazines as a get-well gift, then drove to Patty's home.

Her sister answered the doorbell.

"Hi, you must be from the baseball team. Patty's gotten a lot of company. Everyone's been wonderful."

Abby wasn't surprised. Everyone on the team was warm and friendly.

"This must be her day for company. Come on in. Logan's with her now."

Seven

Abby was dismayed as the sound of Patty's laughter drifted into the entryway, but she followed Patty's sister into the living room.

Patty's broken arm was supported by a white linen sling and she sat opposite Logan on a long sofa. Her eyes were sparkling with undisguised happiness. Logan had his back to Abby, and it was all she could do not to turn around and leave. Instead she forced a bright smile and made an entrance any actress would envy. "Hello, everyone!"

"Hi, Abby!" Patty had never looked happier or, for that matter, prettier. Not only was her hair nicely styled, but she was wearing light makeup, which added color to her pale cheeks and accented her large brown eyes. She wore a lovely summer dress, a little fancy for hanging around the house, and shoes that were obviously new.

"How are you feeling?" Abby prayed the phoniness in her voice had gone undetected.

Logan stood up and came around the couch, but his eyes didn't meet Abby's probing gaze.

"Hello, Logan, good to see you again."

"Hello, Abby."

"Sit down, please." Patty pointed to an empty chair. "We've got a few minutes before dinner." Patty seemed oblivious to the tension between her guests.

"No, thanks," Abby murmured, faking another smile. "I can only stay a minute. I just wanted to drop by and see how you were doing. Oh, these are for you," she said, handing over the magazines. "Some reading material…"

"Thank you! And I'm doing really well," Patty said enthusiastically. "This is the first night I've been able to go out. Logan's taking me to dinner at the Sofitel."

Abby breathed in sharply and clenched her fist until her nails cut into her hand. Logan had taken her there only once, but Abby considered it their special restaurant. He could've taken Patty anyplace else in the world and it would've hurt, but not as much as this.

"Everyone's been great," Patty continued. "Dick and his wife were over yesterday, and a few others from the team dropped by. Those flowers—" she indicated several plants and bouquets "—are from them."

"We all feel terrible about the accident." Abby made her first honest statement of the visit.

"But it was my own fault," Patty said

as Logan hovered stiffly on the other side of the room.

Abby lowered her eyes, unable to meet the happy glow in Patty's. A crumpled piece of wrapping paper rested on the small table at Patty's side. It was the same paper Logan had used to wrap Abby's birthday gift the day before. He *couldn't* have gotten Patty perfume. He wouldn't dare.

"You look so nice," Abby said. Her pulse quickened. What *had* Logan brought Patty? She thought she recognized that scent.... "Is that a new perfume you're wearing?"

"Yes, as a matter of fact, Logan—"

"Hadn't we better be going?" Logan said as he made a show of glancing at his watch.

Patty looked flustered. "Is it time already?"

Following her cue, Abby glared at Logan and took a step in retreat. "I should go, too." A contrived smile curved her mouth. "Have a good time."

"I'll walk you to your car," Logan volunteered.

Walking backward Abby gestured with her hands, swinging them at her sides to give a carefree impression. "No, that isn't necessary. Really. I'm capable of finding my own way out."

"Abby," Logan said under his breath.

"Have a wonderful time, you two," Abby continued, her voice slightly high-pitched. "I've only been to the Sofitel once. The food was fantastic, but I can't say much for my date. But I no longer see him. A really ordinary guy, if you know what I mean. And so predictable."

"I'll be right back." Logan directed his comment to Patty and gripped Abby by the elbow.

"Let me go," she seethed.

Logan's grip relaxed once they were outside the house. "Would you let me explain?"

"Explain?" She threw the word in his face. "What could you possibly say? No." She waved her hand in front of his chest. "Don't say a word. I don't want to hear it. Do you understand? Not a word."

"You're being irrational again," Logan accused, apparently having difficulty keeping his rising temper in check.

"You're right," she agreed. "I've completely lost my sense. Please forgive me for being so closed-minded." Her voice was surprisingly even but it didn't disguise the hurt or the feeling of betrayal she was experiencing.

"Abby."

"Don't," she whispered achingly. "Not now. I can't talk now."

"I'll call you later."

She consented with an abrupt nod, but at that point, Abby realized, she would have agreed to anything for the opportunity to escape.

Her hand was shaking so badly that she had trouble sliding the key into the ignition. This was crazy. She felt secure in his love one night and betrayed the next.

Abby didn't go home. The last thing she wanted to do was sit alone on a Saturday night. To kill time, she visited the Mall of America and did some shopping, buying herself a designer outfit that she knew Logan would hate.

The night was dark and overcast as she let herself into the apartment. Hanging the new dress in her closet, Abby acknowledged that spending this much money on one outfit was ridiculous. Her reasons were just as childish. But it didn't matter; she felt a hundred times better.

The phone rang the first time at ten. Abby ignored it. Logan. Of course. When it started ringing at five-minute intervals, she simply unplugged it. There was nothing she had to say to him. When they spoke again, she wanted to feel composed. Tonight was too soon. She wasn't ready yet.

Calm now, she changed into her pajamas and sat on the sofa, brushing her long hair in smooth, even strokes. Reaction would probably set in tomorrow, but for now she was too angry to think.

Half an hour later, someone pressed her buzzer repeatedly. Annoying though it was, she ignored that, too.

When there was a banging at her door, Abby hesitated, then continued with her brushing.

"Come on, Abby, I know you're in there." Logan shouted.

"Go away. I'm not dressed," she called out sweetly.

"Then get dressed."

"No!" she yelled back.

Logan's laugh was breathless and bitter. "Either open up or I'll tear the stupid door off its hinges."

Just the way he said it convinced Abby this wasn't an idle threat. And to think that only a few weeks ago she'd seen Logan as unemotional. Laying her brush aside, she walked to the door and un-latched the safety chain.

"What do you want? How did you get into the building? And for heaven's sake, keep the noise down. You're disturbing the neighbors."

"Some guy from the second floor recognized me and opened the lobby door. And if you don't let me in to talk to you, I'll do a lot more than wake the neighbors."

Abby had never seen Logan display so much passion. Perhaps she should've been thrilled, but she wasn't.

"Did you and Patty have a nice evening?" she asked with heavy sarcasm.

Logan glanced briefly at his hands. "Reasonably nice."

"I apologize if I put a damper on your *date*," she returned with smooth derision. "Believe me, had I known about it, I would never have visited Patty at such an inopportune time. My timing couldn't have been better—or worse, depending on how you look at it."

"Abby," he sighed. "Let me in. Please."

"Not tonight, Logan."

Frustration furrowed his brow. "Tomorrow, then?"

"Tomorrow," she agreed and started to close the door. "Logan," she called and he immediately turned back. "Without meaning to sound like I care a whole lot, let me ask you something. Why did you give Patty the same perfume as me?" Some perverse part of herself had to know.

His look was filled with defeat. "It seemed the thing to do. I knew she'd enjoy it, and to be honest, I felt sorry for her. Patty needs someone."

Abby's chin quivered as the hurt coursed through her. Pride dictated that she maintain a level gaze. "Thank you for not lying," she said and closed the door.

Tate was waiting for her when Abby entered the park at eleven-thirty Sunday morning. Since her Saturday sessions with Mai-Ling had come to an end, Abby was now devoting extra time on weekends to Tate.

"You look like you just stepped out of the dentist's chair," Tate said, studying her closely. "What's the matter? Didn't you sleep well last night?"

She hadn't.

"You work too hard," he told her. "You're always helping others. Me and Mai-Ling…"

Abby sat on the blanket Tate had spread out on the grass and lowered her gaze so that her hair fell forward, hiding her face. "I don't do nearly enough," she disagreed. "Tate," she said, raising her eyes to his. "I've never told anyone the reason we meet. Would you mind if I did? Just one person?"

Unable to sleep, Abby had considered the various reasons Logan might have asked Patty out for dinner. She was sure he hadn't purposely meant to hurt her.

The only logical explanation was that he wanted her to experience the same feelings he had, since she was continuing to see Tate. And yet he'd gone to pains to keep her from knowing about their date. Nothing made sense anymore. But if she could tell Logan the reason she was meeting Tate, things would be easier....

Tate rubbed a weary hand over his eyes. "This is causing problems with you and—what's-his-name—isn't it?"

Abby didn't want to put any unnecessary pressure on Tate so she shrugged her shoulders, hoping to give the impression of indifference. "A little. But I don't think Logan really understands."

"Is it absolutely necessary that he know?"

"No, I guess not." Abby had realized it would be extremely difficult for Tate to let anyone else learn about his inability to read—especially Logan.

"Then would it be too selfish of me to

ask that you don't say anything?" Tate asked. "At least not yet?" A look of pain flashed over his face, and Abby understood anew how hard it was for him to talk about his problem. "I suppose it's a matter of pride."

Abby's smile relaxed her tense mouth. The relationship among the three of them was a mixed-up matter of pride, and she didn't know whose was the most unyielding.

"No, I don't mind," she replied, and opened her backpack to take out some books. "By the way, I want to give you something." She handed him three of her favorite Dick Francis books. "These are classics in the mystery genre. They may be a bit difficult for you in the beginning, but I think you'll enjoy them."

Tate turned the paperback copy of *The Danger* over and read the back cover blurb. "His business is kidnapping?" He sounded unsure as he raised his eyes to hers.

"Trust me. It's good."

"I'll give it a try. But it looks like it'll take me a while."

"Practice makes perfect."

Tate laughed in the low, lazy manner she enjoyed so much. "I've never known anyone who has an automatic comeback the way you do." He took a cold can of soda and tossed it to her. "Let's drink to your wit."

"And have a celebration of words." She settled her back against the trunk of a massive elm and closed her eyes as Tate haltingly read the first lines of the book she'd given him. It seemed impossible that only a few weeks before he'd been unable to identify the letters of the alphabet. But his difficulty wasn't attributed to any learning disability, such as she'd encountered in the past with others. He was already at a junior level and advancing so quickly she had trouble keeping him in material, which was why she'd started him on a novel. Unfortunately, his writing and spelling skills were advancing at a slower pace. Abby calculated that it wouldn't take more than a month or two before she could set him on his own with the promise to help when he needed it. Already he'd voiced his concerns about an application he'd be filling out for the bank to obtain a business loan. She'd assured him they'd go over it together.

Abby hadn't been home fifteen minutes when Logan showed up at her building. She buzzed him in and opened the door, but for all the emotion he revealed, his face might have been carved in stone.

"Are you going to let me inside today?" he asked, peering into her apartment.

"I suppose I'll have to."

"Not necessarily. You could make a fool of me the way you did last night."

"Me?" she gasped. "You don't need

me to make you look like a fool. You do a bang-up job of it yourself."

His mouth tightened as he stepped into her apartment and sank down on the sofa.

Abby sat as far away from him as possible. "Well?" She was determined not to make this easy.

"Patty was in a lot of pain when I drove her to the hospital the night of the accident," he began.

"Uh-huh." She sympathized with Patty but didn't know why he was bringing this up.

Logan's voice was indifferent. "I was talking to her, trying to take her mind off how much she was hurting. It seems that in all the garble I rashly said I'd take her to dinner."

"I suppose you also—rashly—suggested the Sofitel?" She felt chilled by his aloofness and she wasn't going to let him off lightly.

An awkward silence followed. "I don't

remember that part, but apparently I did."

"Apparently so," she returned with forced calm. "Maybe I could forget the dinner date, but not the perfume. Honestly, Logan, that was a rotten thing to do."

Impatience shadowed his tired features. "It's not what you think. I got her cologne. Not perfume."

"For heaven's sake," she said, exasperated. "Can't you be more original than that?"

"But it's the truth."

"I know that. But you can't go through life giving women perfume and cologne every time the occasion calls for a gift. And, even worse, you chose the same scent!"

"It's the only one I know." He shook his head. "All right, the next time I buy a woman a gift, I'll take you along."

"The next time you buy a woman a

gift," she interrupted in a stern voice, "it had better be me."

He ignored her statement. "Abby, how could you believe I'm attracted to Patty?"

She opened her mouth and closed it again. "Maybe I can believe that you really do care about me. But I've seen the way Patty looks at you. It wouldn't take more than a word to have her fall in love with you. I don't want to see her hurt." Or any of them for that matter, Abby mused. "I don't believe you're using Patty to make me jealous," she said honestly. "I mean, I wondered about it but then decided you weren't."

"I'm glad you realize that much." He breathed out in obvious relief.

"But I recognize the looks she's giving you, Logan. She wants you."

"And Tate wants you!"

Abby's shoulders sagged. "Don't go bringing him into this discussion. It's not right. We were talking about you, not me."

"Why not? Isn't turnabout fair play?" The contempt in his expression made her want to cry.

"That's tiddlywinks, not love," she said saucily.

"But if Patty looks at me with adoring eyes, it only mirrors the way Tate looks at you."

"Now you're being ridiculous," she said, annoyed by his false logic.

Slowly Logan rubbed his chin. "It's always amazed me that you can twist a conversation any way you want."

"That's not true," she said, hating the fact that he'd turned the situation around to suit himself.

"All right, let's put it like this—if you mention Patty Martin, then I mention Tate Harding. That sounds fair to me."

"Fine." She flipped a strand of hair over her shoulder. "I won't mention Patty again."

"Are you still seeing him?"

"Who?" Abby widened her eyes innocently.

Logan's jaw tightened grimly. "I want you to promise me that you won't date Harding again."

Abby stared at him.

"A simple yes or no. That's all I want."

The answer wasn't even difficult. She *wasn't* dating him. "And what do I get in return?"

He bent his head to study his hands. "Something that's been yours for over a year. My heart."

At his words, all of Abby's defensive anger melted. "Oh, Logan," she whispered, emotion bringing a misty happiness to her eyes.

"I've loved you so long, Abby, I can't bear to lose you." There could be no doubt of his sincerity.

"I love you, too."

"Then why are you on the other side

of the room when all I want to do is hold you and kiss you?"

The well of tenderness inside her overflowed. She rose from her sitting position. "In the interests of fairness, I think we should meet halfway. Okay?"

He chuckled as he stood, coming to her, but his eyes revealed a longing that was deep and intense. A low groan rumbled from his throat as he swept her into his arms and held her as if he never wanted to let her go. He kissed her eyes, her cheeks, the corner of her mouth until she moaned and begged for more.

"Abby." His voice was muffled against her hair. "You're not going to sidestep my question?"

"What question?" She smiled against his throat as she gave him nibbling, biting kisses.

His hands gripped her shoulders as he pulled her slightly away from him so he could look into her face. "You won't be seeing Tate again?"

She decided not to make an issue of semantics. He *meant* date, not see. What she said in response was the truth. "I promise never to date anyone else again. Does that satisfy you?"

He linked his hands at the small of her back and smiled deeply into her eyes. "I suppose it'll have to," he said, echoing her remark when she'd let him in.

"Now it's your turn."

"What would you like?"

"No more dating Patty, okay?"

"I agree," he replied without hesitation.

"Inventive gift ideas."

He hesitated. "I'll try."

"You're going to have to do better than that."

"All right, all right, I agree."

"And—"

"There's more?" he interrupted with mock impatience.

"And at some point in our lives I want to drive to Des Moines."

"Fine. Shall we seal this agreement with a kiss?"

"I think it would be only proper," Abby said eagerly as she slid her arms around his waist and fit her body to his.

His large hands framed her face, lifting her lips to meet his. It lacked the urgency of their first kiss, but was filled with promise. His breathing was ragged when he released her, but Abby noted that her own wasn't any calmer.

Not surprisingly, their truce held. Maybe it was because they both wanted it so badly. The next Sunday they met at her place for breakfast, which Abby cooked. Later, they drove over to her parents' house and during their visit Frank Carpenter speculated that the two of them would be married by the end of the year. A few not-so-subtle questions about the "date" popped up here and there in the conversation. But neither of them seemed to mind. Logan was included in Abby's every thought.

This was the way love was supposed to be, Abby mused as they returned to her apartment.

After changing clothes, they rode their bikes to the park and ate a picnic lunch. After that, with Logan's head resting in her lap, Abby leaned against an elm tree and closed her eyes. This was the same tree that had supported her back during more than one reading session with Tate. A guilty sensation attacked the pit of her stomach, but she successfully fended it off.

"Did you hear that Dick Snyder wants to climb Mount Rainier this summer?" Logan asked unexpectedly, as he chewed lazily on a long blade of grass.

In addition to softball, Dick's passion was mountains. She'd heard rumors about his latest venture, but hadn't been all that interested.

"Yeah, I heard that," she murmured. "So?"

"So, what do you think?"

"What do I think about what?" Abby asked.

"They need an extra man. It sounds like the expedition will be cancelled otherwise." Logan frowned as he looked up at her.

"Climbing the highest mountain in Washington State should be a thrill—for some people. They won't have any trouble finding someone. Personally, I have trouble making it over speed bumps," she teased, leaning forward to kiss his forehead. "What's wrong?"

He smiled up at her and raised his hands to direct her mouth to his. "What could possibly be wrong?" he whispered as he moved his mouth onto her lips for a kiss that left her breathless.

The next week was the happiest of Abby's life. Logan saw her daily. Monday they went to dinner at the same Mexican restaurant Tate had taken her to weeks before. The food was good, but Abby's appetite wasn't up to par. Again,

Abby dismissed the twinge of guilt. Tuesday he picked her up for class, but they decided to skip school. Instead they sat in the parking lot and talked until late. From there they drove until they found a café where they could enjoy their drinks outside. The communication between them had never been stronger.

Tate phoned Abby at work on Wednesday and asked her to meet him at the park before the softball game. He wanted to be sure his application for the business loan had been filled out correctly. Uneasy about being in public with him, for fear Logan would see or hear about it, Abby promised to stop off at his garage.

Later, when Logan picked her up for the game she was short-tempered and restless.

"What's the matter with you tonight?" he complained as they reached the park. "You're as jumpy as a bank robber."

"Me?" She feigned innocence. "Nervous about the game, I guess."

"You?" He looked at her with disbelief. "Ms. Confidence? You'd better tell me what's really bothering you. Fess up, kid."

She felt her face heat with a guilty blush. "Nothing's wrong."

"Abby, I thought we'd come a long way recently. Won't you tell me what's bothering you?"

Logan was so sincere that Abby wanted to kick herself. "Nothing. Honest," she lied and tried to swallow the lump in her throat. She hated this deception, no matter how minor it really was.

"Obviously you're not telling the truth," he insisted, and a muscle twitched in his jaw.

"What makes you say that?" She gave him a look of pure innocence.

"Well, for one thing, your face is bright red."

"It's just hot, that's all."

He released a low breath. "Okay, if that's the way you want it."

Patty was in the bleachers when they arrived, and waved eagerly when she saw Logan. Abby doubted she'd noticed that Abby was with him.

"Your girlfriend's here," Abby murmured sarcastically.

"My girlfriend is walking beside me," Logan said. "What's gotten into you lately?"

Abby sighed. "Don't tell me we're going over all of that again?" She didn't wait for him to answer. Instead she ran onto the field, shouting for Dick to pitch her the ball.

The game went smoothly. Patty basked in the attention everyone was giving her and had the team sign her cast. Abby readily agreed to add her own comment, eager to see what Logan had written on the plaster. But she couldn't locate it without being obvious. Maybe he'd done that on purpose. Maybe he'd written Patty a sweet message on the underside of her arm, where no one else could read it. The thought was so ridiculous that Abby almost laughed out loud.

They lost the game by a slim margin, and Abby realized she hadn't been much help. During the get-together at the pizza place afterward she listened to the others joke and laugh. She wanted to join in, but tonight she simply didn't feel like partying.

"Are you feeling all right?" Logan sat beside her, holding her hand. He studied her with worried eyes.

"I'm fine," she answered and managed a halfhearted smile. "But I'm a little tired. Would you mind taking me home?"

"Not at all."

They got up and, with Logan's hand at the small of her back, they made their excuses and left.

The silence in the car was deafening, but Abby did her best to ignore the unspoken questions Logan was sending her way.

"How about if I cook dinner tomorrow?" Abby said brightly. "I've been terrible tonight and I want to make it up to you."

"If you're not feeling well, maybe you should wait."

"I'm fine. Just don't expect anything more complicated than hot dogs on a bun." She was teasing and Logan knew it.

He parked outside her building and kissed her gently. Abby held on to him compulsively as if she couldn't bear to let him go. She felt caught in a game of cat and mouse between Tate and Logan—a game in which she was quickly becoming the loser.

The following evening, Abby was putting the finishing touches on a salad when Logan came over.

"Surprise," he said as he held out a small bouquet of flowers. "Is this more original than perfume?" he asked with laughing eyes.

"Hardly." She gave him a soft brushing kiss across his freshly shaven cheek as she took the carnations from his hand. "Mmm, you smell good."

Logan picked a tomato slice out of the salad and popped it into his mouth. "So do you."

"Well, if you don't like the fragrance, you have only yourself to blame."

"Me? You smell like pork chops." He slipped his arms around her waist from behind and nuzzled her neck. "You know I could get used to having dinner with you every single night." The teasing quality left his eyes.

Abby dropped her gaze as her heart went skyrocketing into space. She knew what he was saying. The question had entered her mind several times during the past few days. These feelings they were experiencing were the kind to last a lifetime. Abby wanted to share Logan's life. The desire to wake up with him at her side every morning, to marry him and have his children, was stronger than any instinct. She loved this man and wanted to be with him always.

"I think I could get used to that, too," she admitted softly.

Someone knocked at the door, breaking into their conversation. Impatiently Logan glanced at it. "Are you expecting anyone? One of your neighbors?"

"You," she said. "Here, turn these. I'll see who it is and get rid of them." She handed him the spatula.

Abby's hand was shaking as she grasped the knob, praying it wouldn't be Tate. If she was lucky, she could ask him to leave before Logan knew what was happening.

Her worst fears were realized when she pulled the door open halfway.

"Hi. Someone let me into the lobby."

"Hello, how are you?" she asked in a hushed whisper.

"I'm returning the books you lent me. I really enjoyed them." Tate gave her a funny look. "Is this a bad time or something?"

"You might say that," she breathed. "Could you come back tomorrow?"

"Sure, no problem. Is it Logan?"

Abby nodded, and as she did, the door was opened all the way.

"Hello, Tate," Logan greeted him stiffly. "I've been half-expecting you. Why don't you come inside where we can all visit?"

Eight

The two men regarded each other with open hostility.

Glancing from one to the other, Abby paused to swallow a lump of apprehension. Her worst fears had become reality. She wanted to blurt out the truth, explain to Logan exactly why she was seeing Tate. But one look at the two of them standing on either side of the door and Abby recognized the impossibility of making any kind of explanation. Like rival warlords, the two blatantly dared each other to make the first move.

Logan loomed at her side exuding bitterness, surprise, hurt and anger. He held himself still and rigid.

"I'll see you tomorrow, Abby?" Tate spoke at last, making the statement a question.

"Fine." Abby managed to find her voice, which was low and urgent. She wanted to scream at him to leave. If pride wasn't dominating his actions, he'd recognize what a horrible position he was putting her in. Apparently maintaining his pride was more important than the problem he was causing her. Abby's eyes pleaded with Tate, but either he chose to ignore the silent entreaty or he didn't understand what she was asking.

The enigmatic look on Tate's face moved from Logan to Abby. "Will you be all right? Do you want me to stay?"

"Yes. No!" She nearly shouted with frustration. He'd read the look in her eyes as a plea for help. This was crazy. This whole situation was unreal.

"Tomorrow, then," Tate said as he took a step in retreat.

"Tomorrow," Abby confirmed and gestured with her hand, begging him to leave.

He turned and stalked away.

Immobile, Abby stood where she was, waiting for Logan's backlash.

"How long have you been seeing each other?" he asked with infuriating calm.

If he'd shouted and decried her actions, Abby would have felt better; she could have responded the same way. But his composed manner relayed far more adequately the extent of his anger.

"How long, Abby?" he repeated.

Her chin trembled and she shrugged.

His short laugh was derisive. "Your answer says quite a bit."

"It's not what you think," she said hoarsely, desperately wanting to set everything straight.

His jaw tightened forbiddingly. "I suppose you're going to tell me you and Tate are just good friends. If that's the case, you can save your breath."

"Logan." Fighting back tears of frustration, Abby moved away from the door and turned to face him. "I need you to trust me in this."

"Trust you!" His laugh was mocking. "I asked you to decide which one of us you wanted. You claimed you'd made your decision. You even went so far as to assure me you wouldn't be seeing Tate again." The intense anger darkened the shadows across his face, making the curve of his jaw look sharp and abrupt.

"I said I wouldn't *date* him again," she corrected.

"Don't play word games with me," he threw back at her. "You knew what I meant."

She merely shook her head, incapable of arguing. Why *couldn't* he trust her? Why hadn't Tate just *told* him? Why, why, why.

"I suspected something yesterday

at the game," Logan continued wryly. "That guilty look was in your eyes again. But I didn't want to believe what I was seeing."

Abby lowered her gaze at the onrush of pain. This deception hadn't been easy for her. But she was bound by her promise to Tate. She couldn't explain the circumstances of their meetings to Logan; only Tate's permission would allow her to do that. But Tate couldn't risk his pride to that extent and she wouldn't ask him to.

Logan's short laugh was bitter with irony. "Yet, when the doorbell rang, I knew immediately it was Tate. To be honest, I was almost glad, because it clears away the doubts in my mind."

Determinedly he started for the door, but Abby's hand delayed him. "Don't go," she whispered. "Please." Her fingers tightened around his arm, wanting to bind him to her forever, beginning with this moment. "I love you and...and if you love me, then you'll trust me."

"Love?" he repeated in a contemptuous voice. "You don't know the meaning of the word."

Stunned, Abby dropped her hand and with a supreme effort met his gaze without emotion. "If that's what you think, maybe it would be better if you did leave."

Logan paused, his troubled expression revealing the inner storm raging within him.

"I may be wrong, but I was brought up to believe that love between two people required mutual trust," Abby added.

One corner of his mouth quirked upward. "And I assumed, erroneously it seems, that love required honesty."

"I...I bent the truth a little."

"Why?" he demanded. "No." He stopped her from explaining. "I don't want to know. Because it's over. I told you before that I wouldn't be kept dangling like a schoolboy while you made up your mind."

"But I *can't* explain now! I may never be able to tell you why."

"It doesn't matter, Abby, it's over," Logan said starkly, his expression impassive.

Abby's stomach lurched with shock and disbelief. Logan didn't mean that. He wouldn't do that to them.

Without another word he walked from the room. The door slammed as he left the apartment. He didn't hesitate or look back.

Abby held out her hand in a weak gesture that pleaded with him to turn around, to trust her. But he couldn't see her, and she doubted it would've had any effect on him if he had. Unshed tears were dammed in her throat, but Abby held her head up in a defiant gesture of pride. The pretense was important for the moment, as she calmly moved into the kitchen and turned off the stove.

Only fifteen minutes before, she had stared lovingly into Logan's eyes, letting her own eyes tell him how much she wanted to share his life. Now, swiftly and without apparent concern, Logan had rejected her as carelessly and thoughtlessly as he would an old pair of shoes. Yet Abby knew that wasn't true. He *did* love her. He couldn't hold her and kiss her the way he did without loving her. Abby knew him as well as he knew her. But then, Abby mused, she had reason to doubt that Logan knew her at all.

Even worse was the fact that Abby recognized she was wrong. Logan deserved an explanation. But her hands were bound by her promise to Tate. And Tate had no idea what that pledge was doing to her and to her relationship with Logan. She couldn't believe he'd purposely do this, but Tate was caught in his own trap. He viewed her as his friend and trusted teacher. He felt fiercely protective of her, wanting in his own way to repay her for the second chance she was giving him by teaching him to read.

Logan and Tate had disliked each other on sight. The friction between them wasn't completely her fault, Abby realized. The ironic part was that for all their outward differences they were actually quite a bit alike.

When Abby had first met Tate that day in the park she'd found him compelling. She'd been magnetically drawn to the same strength that had unconsciously bound her to Logan. This insight had taken Abby weeks to discover, but it had come too late.

The weekend arrived in a haze of emotional pain. Tate phoned Friday afternoon to tell her he wouldn't be able to meet her on Saturday because he was going to the bank to sign the final papers for his loan. He invited her to dinner in celebration, but she declined. Not meeting him gave Abby a reprieve. She wasn't up to facing anyone right now. But each minute, each hour, the hurt grew less intense and life became more bearable. At least, that was what she tried to tell herself.

She didn't see Logan on Sunday, and forced herself not to search for him in the crowded park as she took a late-afternoon stroll. This was supposed to be their day. Now it looked as if there wouldn't be any more lazy Sunday afternoons for them.

Involved in her melancholy thoughts, Abby wandered the paths and trails of the park, hardly noticing the people around her.

Early that evening, as the sun was lowering in a purple sky, Abby felt the urge to sit on the damp earth and take in the beauty of the world around her. She needed the tranquillity of the moment and the assurance that another day had come and gone and she'd made it through the sadness and uncertainty. She reflected on her feelings and actions, admitting she'd often been headstrong and at times insensitive. But she was learning, and although the pain of that growth dominated her mind now, it, too, would fade. Abby stared at the darkening sky and, for the first time in several long days, a sense of peace settled over her.

Sitting on the lush grass, enjoying the richness of the park grounds, Abby gazed up at the sky. These rare, peaceful minutes soothed her soul and quieted her troubled heart. If she were never to see Logan again, she'd always be glad for the good year they'd shared. Too late she'd come to realize all that Logan meant to her. She'd carelessly tossed his love aside—with agonizing consequences.

The following afternoon Abby called Dick Snyder about Wednesday's softball game. Although she was dying for the sight of Logan, it would be an uncomfortable situation for both of them.

"Dick, it's Abby," she said when he answered. She suddenly felt awkward and uneasy.

"Abby," Dick greeted her cheerfully. "It's good to hear from you. What's up?"

An involuntary smile touched the corners of her mouth. No-nonsense Dick. He climbed mountains, coached softball teams, ran a business with the effectiveness of a tycoon and raised a family; it was all in a day's work, as he often said. "Nothing much, but I wanted you to know I won't be able to make the game on Wednesday."

"You, too?"

"Pardon?" Abby didn't know what he meant.

"Logan phoned earlier and said he wouldn't be at the game, either. Are you two up to something we should know about?" he teased. "Like running off and getting married?"

Abby felt the color flow out of her face, and her heart raced. "No," she breathed, hardly able to find her voice. "That's not it at all."

Her hand was trembling when she replaced the receiver a couple of minutes later. So Logan had decided not to play on Wednesday. If he was quitting softball, she could assume he'd also stop attending classes on Tuesday nights. The possibility of their running into each other at work was still present, since their offices were only half a block apart, but he must be going out of his way to avoid any possible meeting. For that matter, she was doing the same thing.

Soon Abby's apartment began to feel like her prison. She did everything she could to take her mind off Logan, but as the weeks progressed, it became more and more difficult. Much as she didn't want to talk to anyone or provide long explanations about Logan's absence, Abby couldn't tolerate another night alone. She had to get out. So after work the following Wednesday, she got in her car and started to drive.

Before she realized where she was headed, Abby pulled into her parents' driveway.

"Hi, Mom," Abby said as she let herself in the front door.

Her father was reading the paper, and Abby paused at his side. She placed her hand on his shoulder, kissing him lightly on the forehead. "What's that for?" Frank Carpenter grumbled as his arm curved around her waist. "Do you need a loan?"

"Nope," Abby said with forced cheer. "I was just thinking that I don't say *I love you* nearly enough." She glanced up at her mother. "I'm fortunate to have such good parents."

"How sweet," Glenna murmured softly, but her eyes were clouded with obvious worry. "Is everything all right?"

Abby restrained the compulsion to cry out that *nothing* was right anymore.

Not without Logan. She left almost as quickly as she'd come, making an excuse about hurrying home to feed Dano. That weak explanation hadn't fooled her perceptive mother. Abby was grateful Glenna didn't pry.

Another week passed and Abby didn't see Logan. Not that she'd expected to. He was avoiding her as determinedly as she did him. Seeing him would only mean pain. She lost weight, and the dark circles under her eyes testified to her inability to sleep.

Sunday morning, Abby headed straight for the park, intent on finding Logan. Even a glimpse would ease the pain she'd suffered without him. She wondered if his face would reveal any of the same torment she had endured. Surely he regretted his lack of trust. He must miss her—perhaps even enough to set aside their differences and talk to her. And if he did, Abby knew she'd readily respond. She imagined the possible scenes that might play out—from complete acceptance on his part to total rejection.

There was a certain irony in her predicament. Tate had been exceptionally busy and she hadn't tutored him at all that week. He was doing so well now that it wouldn't be more than a month before he'd be reading and writing at an adult level. Once he'd completed the lessons, Abby doubted she'd see him very often, despite the friendship that had developed between them. They had little in common and Tate had placed her on such a high pedestal that Abby didn't think he'd ever truly see her as a woman. He saw her as his rescuer, his salvation—not a position Abby felt she deserved.

She sat near the front entrance of the park so she wouldn't miss Logan if he showed up. She made a pretense of reading, but her eyes followed each person entering the park. By noon, she'd been waiting for three hours and Logan had yet to arrive. Abby felt sick with disappointment. Logan came to the park every Sunday morning. Certainly he wouldn't change that, too—would he?

Defeated, Abby closed her book and meandered down the path. She'd been sitting there since nine, so she was sure she hadn't missed him. As she strolled through the park, Abby saw several people she knew and paused to wave but walked on, not wanting to be drawn into conversation.

Dick Snyder's wife was there with her two school-aged children. She called out Abby's name.

"Hi! Come on over and join me. It'll be nice to have an adult to talk to for a while." Betty Snyder chatted easily, patting an empty space on the park bench. "I keep telling Dick that one of these days *I'm* going mountain climbing and leaving him with the kids." Her smile was bright.

Abby sat on the bench beside Betty,

deciding she could do with a little conversation herself. "Is he at it again?" she asked, already knowing the answer. Dick thrived on challenge. Abby couldn't understand how anyone could climb anything. Heights bothered her too much. She remembered once—

"Dick and Logan."

"Logan?" His name cut into her thoughts and a tightness twisted her stomach. "He's not climbing, is he?" She didn't even try to hide the alarm in her voice. Logan was no mountaineer! Oh, he enjoyed a hike in the woods, but he'd never shown any interest in conquering anything higher than a sand dune.

Betty looked at her in surprise. She'd obviously assumed Abby would know who Logan was with and what he was up to.

"Well, yes," Betty hedged. "I thought you knew. The Rainier climb is in two weeks."

"No, I didn't." Abby swallowed. "Logan hasn't said anything."

"He was probably waiting until he'd finished learning the basics from Dick."

"Probably," Abby replied weakly, her voice fading as terror overwhelmed her. Logan climbing mountains? With a dignity she didn't realize she possessed, Abby met Betty's gaze head-on. It would sound ridiculous to tell Betty that this latest adventure had slipped Logan's mind. The fact was, Abby knew it hadn't. She recalled Logan's telling her that Dick was looking for an extra climber. But he hadn't said it as though he was considering it *himself.*

Betty continued, apparently trying to fill the stunned silence. "You don't need to worry. Dick's a good climber. I'd go crazy if he weren't. I have complete and utter confidence in him. You shouldn't worry about Logan. He and Dick have been spending a lot of time together pre-

paring for this. Rainier is an excellent
climb for a first ascent."

Abby heard almost nothing of Betty's pep talk and her heart sank. This
had to be some cruel hoax. Logan was
an accountant. He didn't have the physical endurance needed to ascend four-
teen thousand feet. He wasn't qualified
to do any kind of climbing, let alone a
whole mountain. Someone else should
go. Not Logan.

Not the man she loved.

Betty's two rambunctious boys returned and closed around the women,
chatting excitedly about a squirrel they'd
seen. The minute she could do so po-
litely, Abby slipped away from the family and hurried out of the park. She had
to get to Logan—talk some sense into
him.

Abby returned to her apartment and
got in her car. She drove around, dredg-
ing up the nerve to confront Logan.
If he was out practicing with Dick, he

wouldn't be back until dark. Twice she drove by his place, but his parking space was empty.

After a frustrating hour in a shopping mall, Abby sat through a boring movie and immediately drove back to Logan's. For the third time she saw that he hadn't returned. She drove around again—for how long she was unsure.

Abby couldn't comprehend what had made him decide to do this. A hasty decision wasn't like him. She wondered if this crazy mountain-climbing expedition was his way of punishing her; if so, he'd succeeded beyond his expectations. The only thing left to do was confront him.

Abby drove back to Logan's building, telling herself that the sooner they got this settled, the better. Relief washed over her at the familiar sight of his car.

She pressed his apartment buzzer, but Logan didn't respond. She tried again, keeping her finger on it for at least a minute. And still Logan didn't answer.

Abby decided she could sit this out if he could. Logan wasn't fooling her. He was there.

When he finally answered and let her into the building lobby, Abby ran in, rushing up to his third-floor apartment. He'd opened the door and she stumbled ungracefully across the threshold. Regaining her balance—and her breath—she turned to glare angrily at him.

"Abby." Logan was holding a pair of headphones. "Were you waiting long?" He closed the door, placing the headset on a shelf. "I'm sorry I didn't hear you, but I was listening to a CD."

Regaining her composure, Abby straightened. "Now listen here, Logan Fletcher." She punctuated her speech with a finger pointed at him. "I know why you're doing this, and I won't let you."

"Abby, listen." He murmured her name in the soft way she loved.

"No," she cried. "I *won't* listen!"

He held her away from him, one hand on each shoulder. Abby didn't know if this was meant to comfort her or to keep her out of his arms. Desperately she wanted his arms around her, craved the comfort she knew was waiting for her there.

"You don't need to prove anything to me," she continued, her voice gaining in volume and intensity. "I love you just the way you are. Logan, you're more of a hero than any man I know, and I can't—no," she corrected emotionally, "I *won't* let you do this."

"Do what?"

She looked at him in stunned disbelief. "Climb that stupid mountain."

"So you did hear." He sighed. "I was hoping none of this would get back to you."

"Logan," she gasped. "You weren't planning to let me know? You're doing this to prove some egotistical point to me and you weren't even going to let me

know until it was too late? I can't believe
you'd do that. I simply can't believe it.
You've always been so logical and all of
a sudden you're falling off the deep end."

Now it was his turn to look flabber-
gasted. "Abby, sit down. You're becoming irrational."

"I am not," she denied hotly, but she
did as he suggested. "Logan, please listen to me. You can't go traipsing off to
Washington on this wild scheme. The
whole idea is ludicrous. Crazy!"

He knelt beside her and she framed his
face with both hands, her eyes pleading
with his.

"Don't you understand?" she said.
"You've never climbed before. You need
experience, endurance and sheer nerve
to take on a mountain. You don't have
to prove anything to me. I love you just
the way you are. Please don't do this."

"Abby," Logan said sternly and pulled
her hand free, holding her fingers against
his chest. "This decision is mine. You

have nothing to do with it. I'm sorry this upsets you, but I'm doing something I've wanted to do for years."

"Haven't you listened to a word I've said?" She yanked her hands away and took in several deep breaths. "You could be killed!"

"You seem to be confusing the issues. My desire to make this climb with Dick and his friends has nothing to do with you."

"Nothing to do with me?" she repeated frantically. Had Logan gone mad? "If you think for one instant that I'm going to let you do this, then you don't know me, Logan Fletcher."

He stood up, and smoothed the side of his hair with one hand as he regarded her quizzically. "You seem to be under the mistaken impression that I'm doing this to prove something to you."

"You may not have admitted it to yourself, but that's exactly the reason you are." She shook her head frantically.

"You're climbing this crazy mountain because you want to impress me."

Logan's short laugh was filled with amusement. "I'm doing this, Abby, because I want to. My reasons are as simple as that. You're making it sound like I'm going in front of a firing squad. Dick's an experienced climber. I expect to be perfectly safe," he said matter-of-factly.

"I don't believe you could be so naive," she told him flatly, "about the danger of mountain-climbing *or* about your own motivations."

"Then that's your problem."

"But…you could end up dead!"

"I could walk across the street and be hit by a car tomorrow," Logan replied with infuriating calm.

Abby couldn't stand his quiet confidence another second. She leaped to her feet and stalked across the floor, gesturing wildly with her hands, unable to clarify her thoughts enough to reason with him. Pausing, she took a moment to compose herself. "If this is something you always wanted to do, how come I've never heard about it before?"

"Because I knew what your reaction would be—and I was right. I—"

"You're so caught up in the excitement of this adventure, you can't see how crazy it is," Abby interrupted, not wanting him to argue with her. He *had* to listen.

Logan took her gently by the shoulders and turned her around. "I think you should realize that nothing you say is going to change my mind."

"I drove you to this—" Her voice throbbed painfully.

"No," he cut in abruptly and brushed a hand across his face. "As I keep telling you, this is something I've always wanted to do, whether you like it or not."

"I don't like it and I don't believe it."

"That's too bad." Logan breathed in harshly. "But unlike certain people I know, I don't bend the truth. It's true, Abby."

Abby's mouth twisted in a smile. "And you weren't even going to tell me."

His look was grudging. "I think you can understand why."

Abby shut her eyes and groaned inwardly.

"Now if you'll excuse me, I really do need to get back to the audio book I'm listening to. It's on climbing. Dick recommended it."

"I thought you were smarter than this. I've never heard of anything so stupid in my life," she said waspishly, lashing out at him in her pain.

His smile was mirthless as if he'd expected that kind of statement from her.

"I'm sorry," she mumbled as she studied the scuffed-up toe of her shoe. The entire day had been crazy. "I didn't mean that."

A finger under her chin lifted her eyes to his. "I know you didn't." For that instant all time came to a halt. His eyes burned into hers with an intensity that stole her breath.

Seemingly of their own volition, her hands slid over his chest. She wound her arms around his neck and stood on the tips of her toes as she fitted her mouth over his. The slow-burning fire of his kiss melted her heart. Every part of her seemed to be vibrantly alive. Her nerves tingled and flared to life.

Angrily Logan broke the kiss. "What's this?" he said harshly. "My last kiss before I face the firing squad?"

"Hardly. I expect you to come back alive." She paused, frowning at him. "If you don't, I swear I'll never forgive you."

He rammed his hands into his pants pockets. Then, as if he couldn't bear to look at her, he stalked to the other side of the room. "If I don't come back, why would it matter? We're not on speaking terms as it is."

From somewhere deep inside her,

Abby found the strength to swallow her pride and smile. "That's something I'd like to change."

"No," he said without meeting her gaze.

"You're not leaving for two weeks. During that time you won't be able to avoid seeing me," she went on. "I don't mind telling you that I plan to use every one of those days to change your mind."

"It won't work, Abby," he murmured.

"I can try. I—"

"What I mean is that I have two weeks before the climb, but we're flying in early to explore several other mountains in the Cascade Range."

"The Cascades?" From school, Abby remembered that parts of the Cascade mountain range in Washington State had never been explored. This made the whole foolish expedition even more frightening.

"My flight leaves tomorrow night."

"No," she mumbled miserably, the taste of defeat filling her.

"There's a whole troop who'll be seeing us off. If you're free, you might want to come, too."

Abby noted that he didn't ask her to come, but merely informed her of what was happening. Sadly she shook her head. "I don't think so, Logan. I refuse to be a part of it. Besides, I'm not keen on tearful farewells and good wishes."

"I won't ask anything from you anymore, Abby."

"That's fine," she returned more flippantly than she intended. Involuntary tears gathered in her eyes. "But you'd better come back to me, Logan Fletcher. That's all I can say."

"I'll be back," he told her confidently.

Not until Abby was halfway home did she realize that Logan hadn't said he was coming back *to her.*

Later that night Abby lay in bed while a kaleidoscope of memories went through her mind. She recalled the most memorable scenes of her year-long relationship with Logan. One thing was clear: she'd been blind and stupid not to have appreciated him, or recognized how much she loved him.

Staring at the blank ceiling, she felt a tear roll from the corner of her eye and fall onto the pillow. Abby was intensely afraid for Logan.

The following afternoon, when Abby let herself into her apartment, the phone was ringing.

Abby's heart hammered in her throat. Maybe Logan was calling to say goodbye. Maybe he'd changed his mind and would ask her to come to the airport after all.

But it was her mother.

"Abby." Glenna's raised voice came over the line. "I just heard that Logan's joining Dick Snyder on his latest climb."

"Yes," Abby confirmed in a shaky voice, wondering how her mother had found out about it. "His plane's leaving in—" she paused to check her watch

"—three hours and fifteen minutes. Not that I care."

"Oh, dear, I was afraid of that. You're taking this hard."

"Me? Why would I?" Abby attempted to sound cool and confident. She didn't want her mother to worry about her. But her voice cracked and she inhaled a quivering breath before she was able to continue. "He's in Dick's capable hands, Mother. All you or I or anyone can do is wait."

The hesitation was only slight. "Sometimes you amaze me, Ab."

"Is that good or bad?" Some of her sense of humor was returning.

"Good," her mother whispered. "It's very good."

The more Abby told herself she wouldn't break down and go to the airport, the more she realized there was nothing that could stop her.

A cold feeling of apprehension crept

up her back and extended all the way to the tips of her fingers as Abby drove. Her hands felt clammy, but that was nothing compared to her stomach. The churning pain was almost more than she could endure. Because she hadn't been able to eat all day, she felt light-headed now.

Abby arrived at the airport and the appropriate concourse in plenty of time to see the small crowd of well-wishers surrounding Dick, Logan and company. They obviously hadn't checked in for their flight. Standing off to one side, Abby chose not to involve herself. She didn't want Logan to know she'd come. Almost everyone from the softball team was there, including Patty. She seemed more quiet and subdued than normal, Abby noted, and was undoubtedly just as worried about Logan's sudden penchant for danger as she herself was.

Once Abby thought Logan was looking into the crowd as if seeking someone. Desperately she wanted to run to him, hold him and kiss him before he left. But she was afraid she'd burst into tears and embarrass them both. Logan wouldn't want that. And her pride wouldn't allow her to show her feelings.

When it came time for Logan and the others to check in and go through security, there was a flurry of embraces, farewells and best wishes. Then almost everyone departed en masse.

Abby waited, studying the departures board until she knew his plane had left.

Nine

Abby rolled out of bed, stumbled into the kitchen and turned on the radio, anxious to hear the weather report. They were in the midst of a July heatwave.

Cradling a cup of coffee in her hands, Abby eyed the calendar. In a few days Logan would be home. Each miserable, apprehensive day brought him closer to her.

Betty Snyder continued to hear regularly from Dick about the group's progress as they trekked over some of the most difficult of the Cascade mountains. Trying not to be obvious, Abby phoned Betty every other day or so, to hear whatever information she could impart. Abby still didn't know the true reasons Logan had joined this venture, but believed they were the wrong ones.

The first week after his departure, Abby received a postcard. She'd laughed and cried and hugged it to her breast. An email would've been nice. Or a phone call. But she'd settle—happily—for a postcard. Crazy, wonderful Logan. Anyone else would have sent her a scene of picturesque Seattle or at least the famous mountain he was about to climb. Not Logan. Instead he sent her a picture of a salmon.

His message was simple:

How are you? Wish you were here.
I saw you at the airport. Thank you
for coming. See you soon.
Love, Logan

Abby treasured the card more than the bottles of expensive French perfume he'd given her. Even when several other people on the team received similar messages, it didn't negate her pleasure. The postcard was tucked in her purse as a constant reminder of Logan. Not that Abby needed anything to jog her memory; Logan was continually in her thoughts. And although the message on the postcard was impersonal, Abby noted that he'd signed it with his love. It was a minor thing, but she held on to it with all her might. Logan did love her, and somehow, some way, they were going to overcome their differences because what they shared was too precious to relinquish.

"Disturbing news out of Washington State for climbers on Mount Rainier..." the radio announced.

Abby felt her knees go weak as she pulled out a kitchen chair and sat down. She immediately turned up the volume.

"An avalanche has buried eleven climbers. The risk of another avalanche is hampering the chances of rescue. Six men from the Minneapolis area were making a southern ascent at the time of the avalanche. Details at the hour."

A slow, sinking sensation attacked Abby as she placed a trembling hand over her mouth.

During the news, the announcer related the sketchy details available about the avalanche and fatalities and concluded the report with the promise of updates as they became available. Abby ran for the TV and turned it to an all-news channel. She heard the same report over and over. Each word struck Abby like a body blow, robbing her lungs of oxygen. Pain constricted her chest. Fear, anger and a hundred emotions she couldn't identify were all swelling violently within her. When the telephone rang, she nearly tumbled off the chair in her rush to answer it.

Please, oh, please don't let this be a

call telling me Logan's dead, her mind screamed. *He promised he'd come back.*

It was Betty Snyder.

"Abby, do you have your radio or TV on?" she asked urgently. Her usual calm manner had evaporated.

"Yes...I know," Abby managed shakily. "Have you heard from Dick?"

"No." Her soft voice trembled. "Abby, the team was making a southern ascent. If they survived the avalanche, there's a possibility they'll be trapped on the mountain for days before a rescue team can reach them." Betty sounded as shocked as Abby.

"We'll know soon if it's them."

"It's not them," Betty continued on a desperate note, striving for humor. "And if it isn't, I'll personally kill Dick for putting me through this. We should hear something soon."

"I hope so."

"Abby," Betty asked with concern, "are you going to be all right?"

"I'll be fine." But hearing the worry in her friend's voice did little to reassure her. "Do you want me to come over? I can take the day off…"

"Dick's mother is coming and she's a handful. You go on to work and I'll call you if I hear from Dick—or anyone."

"Okay." Her friends at the clinic and on the team would need reassurance themselves and Abby could quickly relay whatever messages came through. She'd check her computer regularly for any breaking news.

"Everything's going to work out fine." Betty's tone was low and wavering and Abby realized her friend expected the worst.

The day was a living nightmare; every nerve was stretched taut. With each ring of the office phone her pulse thundered before she could bring it under control and react normally.

Keeping busy was essential for her sanity those first few hours. But by quarter to five she'd managed to settle her emotions. The worst that could've happened was that Logan was dead. The worst. But according to the news, no one from the Minneapolis area was listed among those missing and presumed dead. Abby decided to believe they were fine; there was no need to face any other possibility until necessary.

After work Abby drove directly to Betty's. She hadn't realized how emotionally and physically drained she was until she got there. But she forced herself to relax before entering her friend's home, more for Betty's sake than her own.

"Have you heard anything?" she asked calmly as Betty let her in the front door. She could hear the TV in the background.

"Not a word." Betty studied Abby closely. "Just what's on the news. The hardest part is not knowing."

Abby nodded and bit her bottom lip.

"And the waiting. I won't give up my belief that Logan's alive and well. He must be, because I'm alive and breathing. If anything happened to Logan, I'd know. My heart would know if he was dead." Abby recognized that her logic was questionable, but she expected her friend to understand better than anyone else exactly what she was saying.

"I feel the same thing," Betty confirmed.

Dick's mother had gone home and Abby stayed for a while to keep Betty and the kids company. Then she went to her apartment to change clothes and watch the latest update on TV. The television reporter wasn't able to relate much more than what had been available that morning.

Tate was waiting for her at the little Mexican restaurant where they met occasionally and raised his hand when she entered. They'd arranged this on the weekend, and Abby had decided not to change their plans. She needed the distraction.

Her relationship with Tate had changed in the past weeks. He'd changed. Confident and secure now, he often came to her with minor problems related to the business material he was reading. She was his friend as well as his teacher.

"I didn't know if you'd cancel," Tate said as he pulled out a chair for her. "I heard about the accident on Mount Rainier."

"To be honest, I wasn't sure I should come. But I would've gone crazy sitting at home brooding about it," Abby admitted.

"Any news about Logan?"

Abby released a slow, agonizing breath. "Nothing."

"He'll be fine," Tate said. "If anyone could take care of himself, I'd say it was Logan. He wouldn't have gone if he didn't know what to expect and couldn't protect himself."

Abby was surprised by Tate's insights. She wouldn't have thought that Tate would be so generous in his comments.

"I thought you didn't like Logan." She broached the subject boldly. "It seemed that every time you two were around each other, fireworks went off."

Tate lifted one shoulder in a dismissive shrug. "That's because I didn't like his attitude toward you."

"How's that?"

"You know. He acted like he owned you."

The problem was that he held claim to her heart and it had taken Tate to show Abby how much she loved Logan. Her fingers circled the rim of the glass and she smiled into her water. "In a way he does," she whispered. "Because I love him, and I know he loves me."

Tate picked up the menu and studied it. "I'm beginning to realize that...." he murmured. "Look, I'll try to talk to him, if that'll help."

Abby reached across the table and squeezed his hand "Thanks, Tate."

The waitress approached them. "Are you ready to order?"

Abby glanced at the menu and nodded. "I'll have the cheese enchiladas."

"Make that two," Tate said absently. "No." He paused. "I've changed my mind. I'll have the pork burrito."

Abby tried unsuccessfully to disguise her amusement.

"What's so funny?" Tate asked.

"You. Do you remember the first few times we went out to eat? You always ordered the same thing I did. I'm pleased to see you're not still doing it."

"It became a habit." He paused. "I owe you a great deal, Abby, more than I'll ever be able to repay."

"Nonsense." They were friends, and their friendship had evolved from what it had been in those early days, but his gratitude sometimes made her uncomfortable.

"Maybe this will help show a little of my appreciation." Tate pulled a small package from inside his pocket and handed it to her.

Abby was stunned, her fingers numb as she accepted the beautifully wrapped box. She raised her eyes to his. "Tate, please. This isn't necessary."

"Hush and open your gift," he instructed, obviously enjoying her surprise.

When she pulled the paper away, Abby was even more astonished to see the name of a well-known and expensive jeweler embossed across the top of the case. Her heart was in her throat as she shook her head disbelievingly. "Tate," she began. "I—"

"Open it." An impish light glinted in his eyes.

Slowly she raised the lid to discover a lovely intricately woven gold chain on a bed of blue velvet. Even with her untrained eye, Abby recognized that the chain was of the highest quality. A small cry of undisguised pleasure escaped before she could hold it back.

"Tate!" She could hardly take in its beauty. For the first time in months she found herself utterly speechless.

"Abby?"

"I…I can't believe it. It's beautiful."

"I knew you'd like it."

"Like it! It's the most beautiful necklace I've ever seen. Thank you." Abby smiled at him. "But you shouldn't have. You know that, don't you?"

"If you say so."

"*Now* he's agreeable." Abby smiled as she spoke to the empty chair beside her. "Here, help me put it on."

Tate stood and came around to her side of the table. He took the chain from its plush bed and laid it against the hollow of her throat. Abby bowed her head and lifted the hair from the back of her neck to make it easier for Tate to fasten the necklace.

When he returned to his chair, Abby felt a warm glow. "I still think you shouldn't have done this, but to be honest, I'm glad you did."

"I knew the minute I saw it in the jeweler's window that it was exactly what I was looking for. If you want the truth, I'd been searching for weeks for something special to give you. I want to thank you for everything you've done for me."

Abby didn't think Tate realized what a small part she'd played in his tutoring. He'd done all the real work himself. He was the one who'd sought her out with a need and admitted that need—something he'd never been able to do before, having always hidden his inability. Abby doubted Tate recognized how far he'd come from the day he'd followed her home from the park.

Later, when Abby undressed for bed, she fingered the elegant chain, remembering Tate's promise. Maybe now he'd be willing to explain to Logan why Abby had met with him. The chain represented his willingness to help repair her relationship with Logan. That would be the most significant gift he could possibly give her.

Before leaving for work the next morning, Abby checked the news. Nothing. Then she phoned Betty in case there'd been any calls during the night. There hadn't been, and discouragement sounded in Betty's voice as she promised to phone Abby's office if she heard anything.

At about ten that morning, Abby had just finished updating the chart on a young teen who'd visited the clinic, when she glanced up and saw Betty in the doorway.

Abby straightened and stood immobile, her heart pumping at a furious rate. Suddenly, she went cold with fear. She couldn't move or think. Even breathing became impossible. Betty would've come to the office for only one reason, she thought. Logan was dead.

"Betty," she pleaded in a tortured whisper, "tell me. What is it?"

"He's fine! Everyone is. They were stuck on the slopes an extra night, but made it safely to camp early this morning. I just heard—Dick called me."

Abby closed her eyes and exhaled a breath of pure release. Her heart skipped a beat as she moved across the room. The two women hugged each other fiercely as tears of happiness streaked their faces.

"They're on their way home. The flight will land sometime tomorrow evening. Everyone's planning to meet them at the airport. You'll come, won't you?"

In her anger and pain Abby had refused to see him off with the others... until the last minute. She wouldn't be so stubborn about welcoming him home. Abby doubted she'd be able to resist hurling herself into his arms the instant she saw him. And once she was in his arms, Abby defied anyone to tear her away.

"Abby? You'll come, won't you?" Betty's soft voice broke into her musings.

"I'll be there," Abby replied, as the image of their reunion played in her mind.

"I thought you'd want to be." Her friend gave her a knowing look.

Logan was safe and coming home. Abby's heart leaped with excitement and she waited until it resumed its normal pace before returning to her desk.

"Tonight," Abby explained to Tate at lunch on Thursday. She swallowed a bite of her pastrami sandwich. "Their flight's arriving around nine-thirty. The team's planning a get-together with him and Dick on Friday night. You're invited to attend if you'd like."

"I just might come."

Tate surprised her with his easy acceptance. Abby had issued the invitation thoughtlessly, not expecting Tate to take her up on it. For that matter, it might even have been the wrong thing to do, since Logan would almost certainly be offended.

"I was beginning to wonder if you were ever going to invite me to any of those social functions your team's always having."

"Tate." Abby glanced up in surprise. "I had no idea you wanted to come. I wish you'd said something earlier." Now she felt guilty for having excluded him in the past.

"Sure," Tate chimed in defensively. "They'll take one look at a mechanic and decide they've got something better to do."

"Tate, that's simply not true." And it wasn't. He'd be accepted as would anyone who wished to join them. Plenty of friends and coworkers attended the team's social events.

"It might turn a few heads." Tate expelled his breath as if he found the thought amusing.

"Oh, hardly."

"You don't think so?" he asked hopefully.

Tate's lack of self-confidence was a by-product of his inability to read. Now that reading was no longer a problem, he would gain that new maturity. She was already seeing it evolve in him.

Moonlight flooded the ground. The evening was glorious. Not a cloud could be seen in the crystal-blue sky as it darkened into night. Slowly, Abby released a long, drawn-out sigh. Logan would land in a couple of hours and the world had never been more beautiful. She paused to hum a love ballad playing on the radio, thrilled by the romantic words.

She must have changed her clothes three times, but everything had to be perfect. When Logan saw her at the airport, she wanted to look as close to an angel as anything he would find this side of heaven.

She spent half an hour on her hair and makeup. Nothing satisfied her. Tight-lipped, Abby realized she couldn't suddenly make herself into an extraordinarily beautiful woman. Sad but true. She could only be herself. She dressed in a soft, plum-colored linen suit and a pink silk blouse. Dissatisfied with her hair, Abby pulled it free of the confining pins and brushed it until it shimmered and fell in deep natural waves down the middle of her back. Logan had always loved her hair loose....

A quick glance at her watch showed her that she was ten minutes behind schedule. Grabbing her purse, Abby hurried out to her car—and she noticed that it was running on empty. Everything seemed to be going wrong....

Abby pulled into a service station, splurging on full service for once instead of pumping her own. *Hurry*, she muttered to herself as the teenager took his time.

"Do you want me to check your oil?"

"No, thanks." Abby handed him the correct change, plus a tip. "And don't bother washing the window."

Inhaling deep breaths helped take the edge off her impatience as she merged onto the freeway. A mile later an accident caused a minor slowdown.

By the time she arrived at the airport, her heart was pounding. Checking the arrivals board revealed that Logan's flight was on schedule.

Abby ran down the concourse. Within minutes the team, as well as Karen, Logan's assistant, came into sight.

Warmth stole over Abby as she saw Logan, a large backpack slung over one shoulder. His face was badly sunburned, the skin around his eyes white from his protective eye gear. He looked tanned and more muscular than she could remember. His eyes searched the crowd and paused on her, his look thoughtful and intense.

Abby beamed, wearing her brightest smile. He was so close. Close enough to reach out and touch if it weren't for the people crowding around. Abby's heart swelled with the depth of her love. His own eyes mirrored the longing she was sure he could see in hers. These past weeks were all either of them would need to recognize that they should never be apart again.

Abby edged her way toward him and Dick. The others who'd come to greet Logan were chatting excitedly, but Abby heard none of their conversation. Logan was back! Here. Now. And she loved him. After today he'd never doubt the strength of her feelings again.

In her desire to get to Logan quickly, Abby nearly stumbled over an elderly man. She stopped and apologized profusely, making sure the white-haired gentleman wasn't hurt. As she straightened, she heard someone call out Logan's name.

In shocked disbelief, Abby watched as Patty Martin ran across the room and threw herself dramatically into Logan's arms. He dropped his pack. Sobbing, she clung to him as if he'd returned from the dead. Soon the others gathered around, and Dick and Logan were completely blocked from Abby's view.

The bitter taste of disappointment filled her mouth. Logan should have pushed the others aside and come to her. *Her* arms should be the ones around him. *Her* lips should be the ones kissing his.

Proudly Abby decided she wouldn't fight her way through the throng of well-wishers. If Logan wanted her, then she was here. And he knew it.

But apparently he didn't care. Five minutes later, the small party moved out of the airport and progressed to the parking lot. As far as Abby could tell, Logan hadn't so much as looked around to see where she was.

After all the lonely days of waiting for Logan, Abby had a difficult time deciding if she should attend the party being held at a local buffet restaurant in his and Dick's honor the following evening. If he hadn't come to her at the airport, then what guarantee did she have that he wouldn't shun her a second time? The pain lingered from his first rejection. Abby didn't know if she could bear another one.

To protect her ego on Friday night Abby dressed casually in jeans and a cotton top. She timed her arrival so she wouldn't cause a stir when she entered the restaurant. As she'd expected, and as was fitting, Logan and Dick were the focus of attention while they relived their tales of danger on the high slopes.

Abby filled her plate and took a seat

where she could see Logan. She knew she wouldn't be able to force down any dinner; occasionally she rearranged the food in front of her in a pretence of eating.

Sitting where she was, Abby could observe Logan covertly. Every once in a while he'd glance up and search the room. He seemed to be waiting for someone. Abby would've liked to believe he was looking for her, but she could only speculate. The tension flowed out of her as she witnessed again the strength and vitality he exuded. That experience on the mountain had changed him, just as it had changed her.

Unable to endure being separated any longer, Abby pushed her plate aside and crossed the room to his table. Logan's eyes locked with hers as she approached. Someone was speaking to him, but Abby doubted that Logan heard a word of what was being said.

"Hello, Logan," she said softly. Her

arms hung nervously at her sides. "Welcome home."

"It's good to see you, Abby." His gaze roamed her face lovingly. He didn't need to pull her into his arms for Abby to know what he was feeling. It was all there for her to read. Her doubts, confusion and anxiety were all wiped out in that one moment.

"I'm sorry about what happened at the airport." His hand clasped hers. "There wasn't anything I could do."

Their eyes held as she studied his face. Every line, every groove, was so familiar. "Don't apologize. I understand." Who would've believed a simple touch could cause such a wild array of sensations? Abby felt shaky and weak just being this close to him. A tingling warmth ran up the length of her arm as he gently enclosed her in his embrace.

"Can I see you later?"

"You must be exhausted." She wanted desperately to be with him, but she could wait another day. After all this time, a few more hours wouldn't matter.

"Seeing you again is all the rest I need."

"I'll be here," she promised.

Dick Snyder tapped Logan on the shoulder and led him to the front row of tables. After a few words from Dick about their adventure, Logan stood and thanked everyone for their support. He relayed part of what he'd seen and the group's close brush with death.

The tables of friends and relatives listened enthralled as Logan and Dick spoke. Hearing him talk so casually about their adventures was enough to make Abby's blood run cold. She'd come so close to losing him.

Abby stood apart from Dick and Logan while they shook everyone's hand as they filed out the door and thanked them for coming. When the restaurant began to empty Logan hurried across the room and brought Abby to his side. She wasn't proud of feeling this way, but she was glad Patty hadn't come. Abby was also grateful that Tate had called to say he couldn't make it. In an effort to assure him he'd be welcome another time, Abby invited him to the team picnic scheduled that Sunday in Diamond Lake Park. Tate promised to be there if possible.

Logan led her into the semidarkened parking lot and turned Abby into his arms. There was a tormented look in his eyes as he gazed down on her up-turned face.

"Crazy as it sounds, the whole time we were trapped on that mountain, I was thinking that if I didn't come back alive you'd never forgive me." With infinite tenderness he kissed her.

"I wouldn't have forgiven you," she murmured and smiled up at him in the dim light.

"Abby, I love you," he said. "It took a brush with death to prove how much I wanted to come home to you."

His mouth sought hers and with a joyful cry, Abby wrapped her arms around him and clung. Tears of happiness clouded her eyes as Logan slipped his hands into the length of her hair. He couldn't seem to take enough or give enough as he kissed her again and again. Finally he buried his face in the slope of her neck.

He held her face as he inhaled a steadying breath. "When I saw you across the restaurant tonight, it was all I could do to be polite and stay with the others."

Abby lowered her eyes. "I wasn't sure you wanted to see me."

"You weren't sure?" Logan said disbelievingly. He slid his hands down to rest on the curve of her shoulders. His finger caught on the delicate gold chain and he pulled it up from beneath her blouse.

Abby went completely still. Logan seemed to sense that something wasn't right as his eyes searched hers.

"What's wrong?"

"Nothing."

His eyes fell on the chain. "This is lovely and it's far more expensive than you could afford. Who gave it to you, Abby? Tate?"

Ten

Abby pressed her lips so tightly together that they hurt. "Yes, Tate gave me the necklace."

"You're still seeing him, aren't you?" Logan dropped his hands to his sides and didn't wait for her to respond. "After everything I've said, you still haven't been able to break off this relationship with Tate, have you?"

"Tate has nothing to do with you and me," she insisted, inhaling deeply to hide her frustration. After the long, trying days apart, they *couldn't* argue! Abby wanted to cry out that she loved him and nothing else should matter. She should be able to be friends with a hundred men if she loved only him. Her voice shaking, she attempted to salvage their reunion. "I know this is difficult for you to understand. To be honest, I don't know how I'd feel if you were to continue seeing Patty Martin."

His mouth hardened. "Then maybe I should."

Abby realized Logan was tired and impatient, but an angry retort sprang readily to her lips. "You certainly seem to have a lot in common with Patty—far more than you do with me."

"The last thing I want to do is argue."

"I don't, either. My intention in coming tonight wasn't to defend my actions while you were away. And yes—" she paused to compose herself, knowing her face was flushed "—I did see Tate."

The area became charged with an electricity that seemed to spark and crackle. The atmosphere was heavy and still, pressing down on her like the stagnant air before a thunderstorm.

"I think that says everything I need to know," he said with quiet harshness.

Abby nodded sharply, forcing herself to meet his piercing gaze. "Yes, I suppose it does." She took a step backward.

"It was kind of you to come and welcome me back this evening." A muscle twitched in his jaw. "But as you can imagine, the trip was exhausting. I'd like to go home and sleep for a week."

Abby nodded, trying to appear nonchalant. "Perhaps we can discuss this another time."

Logan shook his head. "There won't be another time, Abby."

"That decision is yours," she said calmly, although her voice trembled with reaction. "Good night, Logan."

"Goodbye, Abby."

Goodbye! She knew what he was saying as plainly as if he'd screamed it at her. Whatever had been between them was now completely over.

"I expect you'll be seeing a lot more of Logan now that he's back," Tate commented from her living room the following afternoon.

Abby brought out a sandwich from the kitchen and handed it to him before taking a seat. "We've decided to let things cool between us," she said with as much aplomb as she could manage. "Cool" was an inadequate word. Their relationship was in Antarctica. They'd accidentally run into each other that morning while Abby was doing some grocery shopping and had exchanged a few stilted sentences. After a minute Abby could think of nothing more to say.

"You know what I think, Tate?" Abby paid an inordinate amount of attention to her sandwich. "I've come to the belief that love is a highly overrated emotion."

"Why?"

Abby didn't need to glance up to see the amusement in Tate's face. Instead she took the first bite of her lunch. How could she explain that from the moment she realized how much she loved Logan, all she'd endured was deep emotional pain. "Never mind," she said at last, regretting that she'd brought it up.

"Abby?" Tate's look was thoughtful.

She leaped to her feet. "I forgot the iced tea." She hurried into the kitchen, hoping Tate would let the subject drop.

"Did I tell you the bank approved my loan?"

Returning with their drinks, Abby grinned. "That's great!"

"They phoned yesterday afternoon. Bessler's pleased, but not half as much as I am. I have a lot to thank you for, Abby."

"I'm so happy for you," Abby said with a quick nod. "You've worked hard and deserve this." Abby knew how relieved Tate was that the loan had gone through. He'd called Abby twice out of pure nerves, just to talk through his doubts.

Tomorrow afternoon they were going to attend the picnic together and although Abby was grateful for Tate's friendship, she didn't want to give her friends the wrong impression. Logan had already jumped to conclusions. There was nothing to say the others wouldn't, too. Tate was a friend—a special friend—but their relationship didn't go beyond that. It couldn't, not when she was in love with Logan.

"Abby," Tate said quietly. "I'm going to talk to him."

Sunday afternoon Abby was preoccupied as she dressed in shorts and a Twins T-shirt for the picnic. She was glad Tate was going with her, glad he'd promised to explain, but she hoped Logan didn't do or say anything to make him uncomfortable.

Logan. The unhappiness weighed down on her heart. Her thoughts were filled with him every waking minute. Even her dreams involved him. This misunderstanding, this lack of trust, had to stop once and for all. From the moment Logan had left for Washington, Abby had longed for Tate to explain the situation and heal her relationship with Logan. She'd assumed that as time went on they'd naturally get back together. Now, just the opposite was proving to be true. With every passing hour, Logan was drifting further and further out of her life. Yet her love was just as strong. Perhaps stronger. Whether Tate went through with his confession and whether it changed things remained to be seen.

Since Tate was meeting her at the park, Abby got there early and found a picnic table for them. When Logan came, he claimed the table directly across from hers and Abby felt the first bit of encouragement since they'd last spoken. As quickly as the feeling came, it vanished. Logan set out a tablecloth and unpacked his cooler without so much as glancing her way. Only a few feet separated her from him, but it felt as if their distance had never been greater. He gave no indication that he'd seen her. Even her weak smile had gone unacknowledged.

Soon they were joined by the others, chatting and laughing. A few men played horseshoes while the women sat and visited. The day was glorious, birds trilled their songs from the tree branches and soft music came from someone's CD player. Busy putting the finishing touches on a salad, Abby sang along with the music. The last thing in the world she felt like doing was singing, but if she didn't, she'd start crying.

Tate arrived and Abby could see by the way he walked that he was nervous. He'd met some of the people at the softball game. Still, he looked surprised when one of the guys called out a greeting. The two men talked for a minute and Tate joined her soon afterward.

"Hi."

"There's no need to be nervous," she said, smiling at him.

"What? Me nervous?" he joked. "They're nice people, aren't they?"

"The best."

"Even Logan?"

"Especially Logan."

Tate was silent for a moment. "Like I said, I'll see what I can do to patch things up between you two."

Unhurriedly, she raised her gaze to his. "I'd appreciate that."

His returning smile told her how difficult revealing his past would be. Abby hated to ask him to do it, but there didn't seem to be any other way.

As he wandered off, Abby laced her fingers tightly and sat there, searching for Logan. He was standing alone with his back to her, staring out over the still, quiet lake.

Abby spread out a blanket between the two picnic tables and lay down on it, pretending to sunbathe. She must have drifted off, because the low-pitched voices of Tate and Logan were what stirred her into wakefulness.

"Seems to me you've got the wrong table," Logan was saying. "Your girlfriend's over there."

"I was hoping we could talk."

"I can't see that there's much to talk about. Abby's made her decision."

The noises that followed suggested that Logan was arranging drinks on the table and ignoring Tate as much as possible. Abby resisted the urge to roll over and see exactly what was happening.

"Abby's a friend," Tate said next. "No more and no less."

"You two keep saying that." Logan sounded bored.

"It's the truth."

"Sure."

There was a rustling sound and faintly

Abby could hear Tate stumbling over the awkward words in the list of ingredients on the side of a soda can.

"What are you doing?" Logan asked.

"Reading," Tate explained. "And for me that's some kind of miracle. You see, until I met Abby here in the park helping Mai-Ling, I couldn't read."

A shocked silence followed his announcement.

"For a lot of reasons, I never properly learned," Tate continued. "Then I found Abby. Until I met her, I didn't know there were good people like her who'd be willing to teach me."

"Abby taught you to read?" Logan was obviously stunned.

"I asked her not to tell anyone. I suppose that was selfish of me in light of what's happened between you two. I don't have any excuse except pride."

Someone called Logan's name and the conversation was abruptly cut off. Minutes later someone else announced that it was time to eat. Abby joined the others, helping where she could. She and Tate were sitting with Dick and Betty when she felt Logan's eyes on her. The conversation around her faded away. The space between them seemed to evaporate as she turned and boldly met his look. In his eyes she read anger, regret and a great deal of inner pain.

When it came time to pack up her things and head home, Abby found Tate surrounded by a group of single women. He glanced up and waved. "I'll call you later," he told her cheerfully, clearly enjoying the attention he was receiving.

"Fine," she assured him. She hadn't gotten as far as the parking lot when Logan caught up with her.

He grabbed her shoulder as he turned her around. The anger she'd thought had been directed inward was now focused on her.

"Why didn't you tell me?" he demanded.

"I couldn't," she said simply. "Tate asked me not to."

"That's no excuse," he began, then paused to inhale a shuddering breath. "All the times I questioned you about meeting Tate, you were tutoring him. The least you could've done was tell me!"

"I already told you Tate was uncomfortable with that. Even now, I don't think you appreciate what it took for him to admit it to you," she explained slowly, enunciating each word so there'd be no misunderstanding. "I was the first person he'd ever told about this problem. It was traumatic for him and I couldn't go around telling others. Surely you can understand that."

"What about me? What about *us?*"

"My hands were tied. I asked you to trust me. A hundred times I pleaded with you to look beyond the obvious."

Logan closed his eyes and emitted a

low groan. "How could I have been so stupid?"

"We've both been stupid and we've both learned valuable lessons. Isn't it time to put all that behind us?" She wanted to tell him again how much she loved him, but something stopped her.

Hands buried deep in his pockets, Logan turned away from her, but not before Abby saw that his eyes were narrowed. The pride in his expression seemed to block her out.

Abby watched in disbelief. The way he was behaving implied that *she'd* been the unreasonable, untrusting one. The more Abby thought about their short conversation as she drove home, the angrier she got.

Pacing her living room, she folded her arms around her waist to ward off a sudden chill. "Of all the nerve," she snapped at Dano who paraded in front of her. The cat shot into her bedroom, smart enough to know when to avoid his mistress.

Yanking her car keys out of her purse, Abby hurried outside. She'd be darned if she'd let Logan end things like this.

His car was in its usual space, and he'd just opened the driver's door. She marched over, standing directly in front of him.

Logan frowned. "What's going on?"

She pointed her index finger at his chest until he backed up against the car.

"Now listen here, Logan Fletcher. I've had about all I can take from you." Every word was punctuated with a jab of her finger.

"Abby? What's the problem?"

"You and that stubborn pride of yours."

"Me?" he shouted in return.

"When we're married, you can bet I won't put up with this kind of behavior."

"Married?" he repeated incredulously. "Who said anything about marriage?"

"I did."

"Doesn't the man usually do the asking?" he said in a sarcastic voice.

"Not necessarily." Some of her anger was dissipating and she began to realize what a fool she was making of herself. "And…and while we're on the subject, you owe me an apology."

"You weren't entirely innocent in any of this."

"All right. I apologize. Does that make it easier on your fragile ego?"

"I also prefer to make my own marriage proposals."

Abby paled and crossed her arms. She wouldn't back down now. "Fine. I'm waiting."

Logan squared his shoulders and cleared his throat. "Abby Carpenter." His voice softened measurably. "I want to express my sincere apology for my behavior these past weeks."

"Months," she inserted with a low breath.

"All right, months," Logan amended. "Although you seem to be rushing the moment, I don't suppose it would do any harm to give you this." He pulled a diamond ring from his pocket.

Abby nearly fell over. Her mouth dropped open and she was speechless as he lifted her hand and slipped the solitaire diamond on her ring finger. "I was on my way to your place," he explained as he pulled her into his embrace. "I've loved you for a long time. You know that. I hadn't worked out a plan to steal your heart away from Tate. But you can be assured I wasn't going to let you go without a struggle."

"But I love—"

His lips interrupted her declaration of love. Abby released a small cry of wonder and wound her arms around his neck, giving herself to the kiss as his mouth closed over hers.

Gradually Logan raised his head, and his eyes were filled with the same wonder she was experiencing. "I talked to Tate again after you left the park," Logan said in a husky murmur. "I was a complete fool."

"No more than usual." Her small laugh was breathless.

"I'll need at least thirty years to make it up to you."

"Change that to forty and you've got yourself a deal."

His eyes smiled deeply into hers. "Where would you like to honeymoon?"

Abby's eyes sparkled. "Des Moines—where else?"

* * * * *

The
ESSENTIAL COLLECTION

Shipment One

A Little Bit Country
Country Bride
Wanted: Perfect Partner
Cindy and the Prince
Some Kind of Wonderful
The Courtship of Carol Sommars

Shipment Two

Navy Wife
Navy Blues
Navy Brat
Navy Woman
Navy Baby
Navy Husband

Shipment Three

Yours and Mine
The Bachelor Prince
Denim and Diamonds
The Wyoming Kid
The Man You'll Marry
Marriage Wanted
Laughter in the Rain

Shipment Four

The Cowboy's Lady
The Sheriff Takes a Wife
Marriage of Inconvenience
Stand-In Wife
Bride on the Loose
Same Time, Next Year